Puffin Book

Halfway Across the Galaxy and Turn Left

'I don't think I can bear this exile,' said Mother on the family's second day on planet earth.

'It may not be for as long as we think,' replied X. 'At any moment Lox could beam us saying, "Come home, all is forgiven."'

But it wasn't to be as easy as that. Even with their extraterrestrial powers, learning earth customs caused all sorts of problems for the crazy alien family from Zyrgon.

X, as Family Organizer, tries hard to keep things running smoothly, but with Father's compulsive gambling habits, her little brother's formidable IQ, and her sister's absent-minded powers of levitation – not to mention the unexpected arrival of wild Aunt Hecla in her home-made space raft – who could say what might happen?

Robin Klein was born in Kempsey, New South Wales, Australia, one of nine children. She began writing full time in 1981 and has established herself as one of the most highly respected of today's writers for children.

Other books by Robin Klein

Boss of the Pool
Hating Alison Ashley
People Might Hear You

Halfway Across the Galaxy and Turn Left

Robin Klein

Puffin Books

Puffin Books, Penguin Books Ltd, Harmondsworth, Middlesex, England
Viking Penguin Inc., 40 West 23rd Street, New York, New York 10010, U.S.A.
Penguin Books Australia Ltd, Ringwood, Victoria, Australia
Penguin Books Canada Limited, 2801 John Street, Markham, Ontario, Canada L3R 1B4
Penguin Books (N.Z.) Ltd, 182–190 Wairau Road, Auckland 10, New Zealand

First published in Viking Kestrel by Penguin Books Australia 1985
First published in Puffin Books by Penguin Books Australia 1985
First published in Great Britain in Puffin Books 1987

Copyright © Robin Klein, 1985

Printed and bound in Great Britain by
Cox & Wyman Ltd, Reading

CIP

Klein, Robin, 1936–
Halfway Across the Galaxy and Turn Left.

For children.
ISBN 0 14 03 1843 7.

I. Title
A823′.3

ONE

It was clear from the first moment of landing that Mother's calculations were wrong and X's were correct. Mother had calculated that the family would touch down in eighteenth-century Versailles, and had one little velvet slipper poised, all set to run out and greet it. When she saw the actual landing space/time zone, she collapsed in a spiral of brocade and started yelling.

'Just typical of you, Father, buying a second-hand steerage computer from that shifty character you met at the Zoomtrack! Anyone else would have seen that it was obsolete government property! Oh, I should have known better than to come!' She would have burst into tears of fury, but didn't want to spoil the heart-shaped beauty spots pasted on her cheeks.

Father nonchalantly stepped out of the space raft and picked her a rose, and as they were as rare as black diamonds back home on Zyrgon, Mother relented enough to follow him down the stairs. X felt some sympathy for her, dragged halfway across the galaxy. None of them had wanted to leave home. Qwrk had just been nominated on his fifth solar birthday for a full professorship to the Knowledge Bank, and Dovis was waiting to be auditioned for the Cosmic Fliers. There wasn't anything as glamorous as that binding X to home. She often felt as ordinary as a control button, wedged between those two eminent siblings. However, she had an important reason of her own for not wanting to leave. Lox. She had idolized him for as long as she could remember. Parting, even a temporary one, was anguish, but there was no help for it.

Father had got himself into a spot of trouble in Zyrgon, by inventing a successful, though devious, method of winning the government lottery. He won twenty-seven times in a row and even though he'd always inscribed the tickets with the names of visiting aliens, the authorities became suspicious. Mother couldn't bear the thought of Detention Centre, and there was nowhere to hide where they lived. Zyrgon was a very small planet, and everyone on it knew everyone else. So that was why X, as Family Organizer, made Father spend some of the lottery money on a pre-used raft. She'd also told the neighbours, one jump ahead of the Law Enforcers, that the whole family was going to Zyrgon's second moon to visit Aunt Hecla and her hybrid-antelope stud farm. But instead, they had come halfway across the galaxy and turned left.

'That steerage-computer definitely indicated eighteenth-century Versailles,' Mother said sadly. 'I thought I'd have afternoon refreshments with the French monarchs and dance a minuet.'

'I told you from start to finish that it wouldn't be Versailles,' X said. 'I wish you'd learn to trust MY calculations, which certainly didn't include travelling back into history. Distance was quite hard enough to master, thank you! Wasting all that time on the voyage learning French and making that ridiculous costume!'

She waited impatiently for Qwrk and Dovis to come down the stairs, not allowing any luggage except the store of currency, the necessary official papers, and the

Pocket Information Calculator. Then she utilized all her powers to create an air pocket, and the raft, which had been poised in the middle of the field like a silver ob elisk, vanished, leaving nothing but a semi-circle of fuel leaks on the grass. (That raft, like the steerage-computer, had also been bought from the shady character at the Zoomtrack.)

'Our last link with home gone!' Mother wailed. 'Poor little Qwrk could this minute be attending his very own investiture at the Knowledge Bank! And Dovis having to miss the audition! And my Fifth-Day Luncheon Club! I was going to have everything transparent this time, to show that conceited Mrs Gombaldu a thing or two. Crystal cakes, and the moonchip tumblers I won from saving all the Klickscore coupons . . .'

'She doesn't say anything about MY routine being interrupted,' X thought bleakly. 'But then, I don't have glittering talents like Dovis and Qwrk. There's nothing glamorous about being a Family Organizer.' She thought of a conversation overheard at one of those Fifth-Day Luncheons. 'I've been blessed in my children,' Mother had said to the members. 'Dovis is as beautiful as a triplicate moonrise. Qwrk is a professor at the age of five. Oh, and I've got X, of course. I'd almost forgotten. It's useful, having an Organizer like X in a family.'

But the centre of an alien field was no place for idle reminiscence. 'Mother, stop that noise at once,' X said sternly. 'People down here don't lament in public. We mustn't draw attention to ourselves. Besides, our last link with home is just tucked away temporarily. Now, before we leave this deserted spot to find somewhere to live, everyone must listen to me carefully. I want to remind you that they have Detention Centres down here, also, for

3

people who aren't averse to bending the rules a little.'

Father nodded meekly, on his best behaviour. Dovis wasn't paying heed. She'd found the wild-rose bush beside the landing site and was making herself a coronet.

'You can't wear that,' X said. 'People might stare at you.'

She thought glumly that people probably would stare at Dovis, anyhow, even without the rose coronet. They always did on Zyrgon. Dovis had already had ten betrothal offers even though she was only just into her adolescence. Sometimes flowers sprang into bloom on the ground where she walked. Her hair billowed into golden wings, her voice was like harp music, and she wrote poetry. She was very annoying.

Right now she was treading air to gather roses from the top of the bush.

'Dovis! Stop levitating!' X said, cross with responsibility. 'It was discussed on the voyage, what we can do and what we mustn't.'

Dovis didn't obey straight away, and when she did come down, it was only because she saw a pretty animal in a corner of the field. She went to it and communicated. They knelt eye to eye, telling each other their lives' histories.

X looked across the field to the distant town and its traffic. There were no romantic horses and coaches as her mother had yearned for, but fairly modern traffic much the same as they had at home. Still, she felt an unfamiliar flicker of uneasiness for all the new burdens now placed upon her, even though she'd studied the Pocket Information Calculator so conscientiously during the three-day voyage.

'Ready when you are, X,' Father said cheerfully.

They put such trust in her, were so confident about her abilities! X hid her uneasiness and checked the family's clothes before they entered civilization. During the three days, she had transformed Qwrk's, Dovis's and her own travel overalls into shirts and long dark-blue trousers. That, apparently, was what young people wore down here. Father had rather fancied a suit of thin stripes on a dark background with a bow tie and bi-coloured shoes. He'd seen such a pattern on the PIC and was drawn to it, but X pointed out that it belonged to an earlier period. She'd made him a plain white shirt, grey trousers and tie instead, though he grumbled about his Zyrgonese travel outfit being altered into anything so dull.

Mother hadn't helped much with the clothes preparation. She'd stubbornly insisted that they would arrive in Versailles, and had concentrated on brocade and powdered curls.

'The rest of us look correct, but you don't,' X said. 'Take off that silly garment and make it into a plain dress that no one will notice particularly. You've got a garment repair kit in your handbag, even though I told you not to bring any tools of trade. A plain dress, I said, Mother. No trimmings.'

'All right, then, a plain dress,' Mother said sulkily. 'Plain for mourning. I shall wear nothing else all the time I'm forced to live down here.'

When everyone was ready, X led them out of the field and down the road towards town. The buildings were certainly different from the slender tapering apartment towers on Zyrgon.

'Horizontal instead of vertical,' Father said. 'I don't know that I like it. Countryside shouldn't be cluttered up with housing, and besides, who'd want all that green garden stuff around their apartment? I wouldn't fancy it myself. Any law enforcer could creep up unawares and nab you!'

'Still, it's gracious, I suppose,' said Mother.

'And there would be plenty of room to build your own private planetarium or laboratory,' said Qwrk, impressed. 'I wonder why they don't? All they have are tiled pits full of water diluted with chemicals.'

'Swimming pools,' X said impatiently. 'You should have done more general study on the voyage. I don't want you all bothering me with questions about the names of new things. From now on, you must all look up the PIC data for yourselves.'

Dovis stopped suddenly. 'I don't need any data on that beautiful apartment!' she cried. 'I shall live there! Goodbye, everyone!'

Before X could stop her, she skimmed away from the group and into the grounds of an impressive house. It was clear that a bribe-taking official of some kind lived there. No other person could have afforded it, not even someone like their father with his innovative gambling schemes. X watched in dismay as her sister tried to open the door manually. When that didn't work, Dovis tapped her heels together and used kinetics, showing off a little, as she was more skilled at kinetics than anyone else in the family. The door slid gently open and she waltzed inside. There seemed to be no electronic challenge installed in the house entrance, no relayed voice querying her intentions.

'X, rescue that foolish girl!' cried Mother. 'We don't know what sort of people live in that house! According to the PIC, this planet has always been filled with questionable types. They've never had any really efficient mood control for the problem population.'

'Everyone wait here,' X said, for Father was regarding the house with a definite gleam in his eye, calculating its riches, and she didn't trust him at all.

Dovis had found a mirror in a gilded-metal frame, just inside the doorway. She'd stopped to admire her image, standing quite still, dazzled, as always, by her own beauty. X knew it would be useless to call; whenever Dovis came upon a mirror, you could intone her name till the stars melted before she'd answer or even hear. She hooked her hand in amongst Dovis's long tendrils of hair and tugged her back outside. Dovis came quietly, not being a fighter. None of those Cosmic Flier types were, X thought scornfully.

'You are NEVER to go off like that again by yourself,' she scolded. 'You know very well that we have to stay together in a group. Do you want to jeopardize all my arrangements? You can't just stroll in and out of people's dwellings on this planet.' Dovis, reacting as she always did when scolded, drifted away behind glazed eyes to some secret spot inside her mind.

They walked on until they came to the town's centre.

'This is more like it,' Father said. 'Buildings close together as they should be. Plenty of escape routes over rooftops, and crowds to hide in.'

X noticed that Qwrk had taken out his solar reckoner and was snap-recording the passing vehicles. 'Put that reckoner away at once!' she said sharply. 'I didn't even give you permission to bring it off the raft. The PIC is quite sufficient.' She confiscated the reckoner with a sharp rap over Qwrk's knuckles. It had been a mistake, she thought, to send him to that expensive, professor-orientated Knowledge Bank, instead of to Zyrgon

Community Centre like everyone else's child. Mother had only been trying to impress Mrs Gombaldu, anyhow.

'We must find a house of our own,' she said. 'Look out for a notice saying Real Estate Agent.'

But everyone was too busy gazing at other things. The PIC was passed rapidly from hand to hand as they came upon new and curious sights. X didn't need to consult it very often, and was pleased with herself for learning so much on the voyage. She was, however, unprepared for the noise and disorder. Nothing seemed well planned. There was, for instance, a garment shop next to one selling food, and next to that was one that apparently sold music. A great discordant blare of sound cascaded from the entrance.

It seemed an untidy plan for a shopping centre, and the people were untidy, too, in their movements. Nobody obeyed a code of walking behaviour. For one terrible moment, X was separated from her family by a large bulky woman with a little cart on wheels. When she caught up, Mother was gazing at a shop that displayed clothing. She was a Wear Designer on Zyrgon, and the different materials here interested her very much, though she was scathing about their style. She couldn't quite forgive missing out on romantic Versailles.

Dovis still hadn't emerged from the secret region in her mind, and walked with her eyes fastened upon nothing. X held her tightly by an arm, so that she couldn't absently levitate. People turned to stare at her beauty, but on the whole, X started to relax a little. Her family, she decided, didn't look so very different from the native population.

Halfway along the main street there was a Real Estate Agent. X gazed, bewildered, at the cryptic words under

8

the photographs on display: *WW carps; lge kit; OFP; BIRs; cls all convs.*

'Close all convs?' Mother said. 'What can that mean?'

'Convoys?' suggested Qwrk. 'A house that's close to a space depot, most likely. Let's take that one. I'd like to study their flight techniques while we're here.'

'They still use that smelly old-style fuel,' Mother said disdainfully. 'I haven't come all this way to choke in air-traffic fumes. If I have to live in a sub-standard house in a primitive society . . .'

'They aren't really sub-standard houses, Mother, only different. Some of them look extremely comfortable,' X said. 'And I must hire one before Dovis comes back from her secret mind place. She always complicates decisions so.'

'None of these houses look nearly as nice as Versailles.'

'It doesn't matter where we live. We might hear very soon that we can go back to Zyrgon.'

Mother was beginning to dab at her eyes again, so X hurried everyone through the door of the Estate Agent. 'We wish to lease a house,' she said, not allowing herself to dwell on the fact that she was addressing one of THEM for the first time.

'We have several houses for rent,' the man said, talking over the top of her head to Father.

'An appalling lack of etiquette!' X thought indignantly. He didn't look like a person with minimum manners-training, either, being neatly dressed and prosperous. 'We need a dwelling immediately, one that we can use from today,' X said, but the man scarcely paid any attention to her at all. He talked almost exclusively to her father.

Then he led the family outside and into a large, gleaming vehicle. It looked cumbersome to her eyes, but Qwrk was obviously intrigued by it. Protective instincts rising, X noticed that it apparently had no monitored steering at all, being totally in the charge of this Mr Herring, for that was his name. It seemed an irresponsible state of affairs. She thought of flighty Dovis given charge of such an uncontrolled vehicle, or Qwrk, with his mind that was apt to explode into spasmodic white light, swamping everything else he might be doing. And this community must surely have its share of people similar to Qwrk and Dovis, all given freedom to dash about unchecked. It was almost, she thought, as though this town's transport system was one huge Zoomtrack! But Mr Herring, she was pleased to discover, maintained a decorous speed as he took them out of town.

'More countryside that is cluttered up,' Father whispered to her over the back seat. 'I wish they wouldn't do it. It should be one or the other.'

'It's called suburbia,' X said. 'A sort of mid-way state.' She decided that she rather liked the idea of separate housing, each in its neat rectangle of green. It would make quite a pleasant change, not having to share an elevator with forty other household Organizers when you went about your business. You could almost come and go without anyone noticing.

'The streets have names!' said Mother. 'Oh, how endearing, and look at those dear little buildings next to the houses! What are they for? Do people keep strange pets in them?'

'They're called garages,' said X. 'Hush, Mother. Mr Herring will think you're odd if you show you don't know. People here store their vehicles in them.'

'How strange. Don't they have communal under-apartment parking?'

'Sssh!' said X. 'I think this ...ne building for lease that Mr Herring wants us to examine.'

But she saw that it wasn't suitable at all. Although the house was set in its own grounds, the skyline behind was spoiled by massive ugly pylons bearing cables. It would have been impossible to gaze at their distant, real home at night. Each room of that house was like a little dark pit, like the places on Zyrgon where they mined for pearlrock.

'We don't want this one,' she said to Mr Herring, but he was chatting over her head again.

'A marvellous locality, available at this price only because the owner has gone overseas for a year. Plenty of space for a billiard table, bar, rumpus area for the kids, you name it.'

'We don't require any of those things, whatever they are,' X said, raising her voice. 'This house isn't suitable. And surely the building regulations have been contravened? Does the government allow the leasing of houses with great spreading patches of damp?' She pointed out the stains, masked though they were with pigment, and Mr Herring looked at her unpleasantly.

'Coffee stains,' he said. 'And they've been nicely touched up with paint.'

'Damp and mildew,' X said severely. 'Criminally disguised with paint.'

'I wouldn't like my children to live in a damp house,' Mother said. 'And besides, there isn't enough window area. At night we wouldn't be able to look through the sky and see . . .'

'The stars,' X said, treading sharply on her foot. 'We're all interested in astronomy.'

'Then I've got just the place for you out on Panorama Drive,' said Mr Herring. 'Smaller – I mean cosier – but still plenty of room for a hobby telescope.'

He took them to the house on Panorama Drive, which was so awful that even Aunt Hecla wouldn't have considered it as a stable for her hybrids. X pointed out, among many other faults, that the main-room floor had a five-degree slope, and that the chimney needed underpinning. Mr Herring gave her another displeased look.

'Quite a little old lady, your daughter,' he remarked to Mother.

'Oh, no, X is only in her three-hundredth year,' she said, forgetting to convert the Zyrgon lunar years into solar terminology, which made X only twelve. X could see that she was tired from the long voyage and liable to make more mistakes which perhaps couldn't be disguised by coughing.

So when Mr Herring showed them the third house on his list, she said, with just a superficial inspection, 'We'll take this one, please.'

'But you haven't checked for spreading damp, termites, bracing, plumbing, wiring and noise pollution,' Mr Herring said sarcastically.

'This one,' X said. 'Now, the bond money, the advance rent, and the signing of the lease.'

The mention of money made Mr Herring quite spry and he drove them back to his shop at an alarming speed. While he was preparing the official papers, X whispered to Father to get out some of the hidden currency. Father went behind a screen of house pictures and drew out a bundle from his security vest. The currency was of paper, and not very clean, unlike the sparkling disc-money of Zyrgon. Father's dubious friend from the Zoomtrack had obtained it. He often had to retire secretly to this planet for various reasons similar to Father's. X was dismayed to find that half of the money belonged to different countries and eras, some of them lost in time. Father's friend obviously hadn't trusted that steerage computer, either.

She found the correct notes to give to Mr Herring, and after the business transactions were completed, led the family back to the new house. It was a very long walk. The others kept nagging her to let Dovis transport them all there by kinetics, but she wouldn't allow it, because it would have been out of the ordinary and definitely cause people to notice them. When they reached the house, she took charge of the keys and opened the front door. They entered, exhausted. It had been a tremendous strain, this first dealing with the populace. From weariness, Qwrk shed his mental age and became his nasty little chronological one. He started to whine for the chemical analyser which Aunt Hecla had given him for his birthday. X said he couldn't have it, so Qwrk just went away into a corner and fiddled with gravity. There was a noise like a fragmented thunderclap and the analyser slid through a small ragged slit in the wall and settled on the floor of the main room.

'I told you not to transfer possessions here!' X scolded. 'Just look at that hole! Now their weather will get in! Do you expect me to do household repairs when we've been here for only five minutes, you intellectual little pest?'

'I'll run up a batch of molecular-reaction adhesive and fix it,' Qwrk said.

'Oh, no you won't! They don't use repair methods like that here. They go to a place called Hardware and buy renovating materials. We mustn't deviate from their ways at all.'

But she was too tired to go out and find a Hardware. Her eyelids kept sliding shut like airlocks, and Dovis was already fast asleep, floating gently somewhere up near the ceiling. The rest of them not possessing her talent, X relented enough to allow Qwrk to fiddle with gravity again and transfer the travel hammocks from the space-raft. They tumbled into them and into instant sleep.

TWO

At the beginning of the second day, X made a shopping list. Household equipment was needed, for the house was a shell only.

'They have such strange furniture,' Mother said, looking at the PIC.

'Versailles would have been more strange.'

'That would have had the charm of antiquity. This is supposed to be modern, just like Zyrgon, but it's not. It's just inconvenient. I shall have to use all my decorating skills to transform this apartment into a proper place to live.'

'We won't have enough currency for anything beyond essentials.'

'Don't worry, X. If there's not enough money, I shall get a job,' Father offered.

'The very idea, my husband working!' Mother cried indignantly. 'Everyone will think that I'm not capable of supporting a husband! I'll be the one to get a job in this family. If Mrs Gombaldu ever heard that I allowed you to go out to work, she'd ostracize me completely on Fifth-Day Luncheons.'

'It's different here,' X explained. 'Any adult person in a household may work without social discrimination. Although, mind you, I think it's best if Father only appears to work on official documents.'

They breakfasted on the emergency supplies brought from the raft in Mother's handbag. 'That's another thing,' Mother grumbled. 'Now we shall have to get used to their food.'

'We've no choice,' X said. 'I've placed food-buying at the top of my list.'

She went out to shop, taking only Qwrk. The others didn't mind being left. Mother wanted to change the colours of the interior walls, and Dovis needed two hours of intensive exercising to keep her flying-muscles limber. Father had found an old newspaper in one of the empty rooms, its final page devoted to the local gambling pastime. He didn't even hear them leave.

X located a group of shops and she and Qwrk entered one that sold food. X knew basically what to expect, but was startled by the noisiness within that place. Small children wailed and roared and she eyed them with disapproval. 'Even you didn't act like that when you were such an age, and I took you out with me,' she whispered to Qwrk.

'You didn't ever take me to an exciting place like this. I wish you had!'

'It's what they call a supermarket. I don't know why you find it so interesting. The sooner we're out of here, the better, as far as I'm concerned. The PIC says they made a scientific time-and-motion study and decided that this was the most efficient shopping method to suit the population. I don't think it's efficient. It just seems like chaos with a thin veneer of order.'

X took a metal trolley, as everyone else was doing. The wheels made a hideous screeching sound and seemed to possess a will of their own. It was hard to look composed and dignified. 'And such a clumsy method of handling food,' she said critically. 'Just look at it, all in a raw state or sealed in heavy metal canisters!' She thought of the efficiency of Zyrgon, where she just placed a monthly order with the doorkeeper of their apartment tower, and the compressed food slabs, in colour-coded envelopes, were delivered by courier.

'How are we going to carry what we buy back to the house?' Qwrk asked.

X studied the method used by the other customers. They put their supplies in the wheeled trolleys, which they took through a checkout booth. Then they wheeled the trolleys outside to their vehicles for unloading.

'We shall have to wheel ours all the way home,' Qwrk said. 'Oh, we can't. Look at that notice: *Trolleys must not be removed from the car park. Penalty $50.* We'll just have to go and buy a vehicle. I'd like to get one with one of those quaint six-cylinder engines.'

'I have to conserve this money with great care,' X said. 'That other notice says we can have our food supplies delivered by the store personnel. And after we buy the food, we must buy household equipment. Then, and only if we have enough money left, shall I consider a vehicle. I might point out to you that it is I who am in charge of procedure!'

She decided to buy a recipe book as the PIC had instructed. The most efficient method would be for Father to start at the first page and by the end of the book, he would hopefully have mastered the local food preparation methods. She took a recipe book from the stand, wondering how anyone could find time to gain their information by such a slow and old-fashioned method as reading. Then she searched the shelves for the peculiar ingredients listed for recipe one. They were difficult to find in that large place. Qwrk was no help. He was wandering about looking at things.

'Where shall I find a tablespoon of cinnamon?' she asked a shop assistant.

'Tins of cinnamon are over there with the other spices, love.'

'I'm sorry, but you must have mistaken me for someone else you know,' X said, wishing that she had indeed such a pretty name as Love instead of X. But the assistant had gone back to stamping prices on metal canisters and didn't hear. Eventually X found the cinnamon, sugar, apples, flour and butter required for the recipe, and wondered how these strange substances could ever be edible.

'We should have some emergency rations, too,' she said, not really knowing what to buy, but Qwrk helped by making a rapid estimation of which items were being bought by the largest percentage of people. X filled the trolley with the same things and wheeled it through the checkout, putting the items onto the conveyor belt just as the person before her had done. Qwrk, intrigued by the cash register, stood on breathless tiptoe. The operator smiled at him kindly and said, 'School holiday, is it, dear?'

'My name is not Dear, it's Qwrk,' he said, and she looked at him, puzzled. X remembered, annoyed with her oversight, that she hadn't yet arranged new first names for her household. The assistant asked for their address for delivery, and X told her that it was 18, Renmark Street, Bellwood, for that was what had been written on the rental lease.

'What name?' the assistant asked, and X knew that she

meant their family name. She had a fleeting, but alarming mental block. Their real family name was long and complicated, containing as it did their Zyrgonese zone-number, Father's lucky gambling-sign, Mother's Wear Designer and Fifth-Day Luncheon logotypes, Dovis's, Qwrk's and her own birthdates, and Aunt Hecla's signal as next of kin. It wouldn't do at all to give that.

'Jackson,' X said, remembering with relief the name Father had used to sign the house lease. (Lox had suggested Jackson as a good general-purpose family name for most time/space zones on this particular planet.) The store assistant was quite satisfied with it, and wrote it above the address on the box containing the food purchases. X paid, and headed thankfully for the exit door.

'Change, please!' called the assistant.

X stopped. Change into what? She had no other clothes with her. Then she saw the proffered coins, remembered the data and blushed.

'Anyone can make an error,' Qwrk said kindly when they were out on the street. 'There's a great deal to learn, even about simple subjects. I was studying the PIC before anyone got up this morning. I was looking for information about their transport. X, let's go and buy a vehicle now! They still have a choice of manual or automatic gear change here. Let's get manual, so I'll have the chance to drive a vintage vehicle.'

'First the household equipment,' X said. 'Being nominated as a professor has certainly given you a swollen head! I'm tired of reminding you that I'm in charge of running this family!'

She found a store that sold household furniture. It all looked heavy and unwieldy, and she felt sorry for Father, who would have to tackle his daily housework with furniture that couldn't be ceiling-suspended while he dusted.

'I'm not going to sleep in a thing like that,' Qwrk said, inspecting the bedding. 'I'd rather use one of the space-raft hammocks permanently.'

'The hammocks were just for an emergency measure last night. I've already told Dovis to process them back to the raft. We must have exactly the same type of furniture as other people down here, so no arguments from you, please.'

An official approached. 'I wish to buy some beds,' X said. 'I'd also like five chairs and a table, a couch, and some electrical equipment to clean a house.'

'Your parents might be looking for you, little girl,' the man said indulgently. 'Run along and find your mother.' He passed them, not stopping at all, and went to attend to some customers at the far end of the store.

'Such bad manners!' X said furiously. 'But it's my own fault. It's true that parents usually shop for household furniture. I should have remembered after that business with the estate agent. Perhaps we'd better go back to the house and fetch Mother.'

She and Qwrk looked at each other soberly, knowing that Mother couldn't be trusted in shops. She loved new possessions and would cheerfully zip right through any amount of currency. And if she couldn't afford something she liked, she wasn't above talking Father into going back later and stealing it for her. Or even employing Dovis's talents.

'Shopping here is complicated,' X said. 'Qwrk, I want you to concentrate very hard and become middle-aged with me.'

The instant, simulated-aged state was a success. X was

pleased, for she'd studied that subject for only one term at Community Centre, and Qwrk hadn't ever studied it at all, considering it to be not intellectually challenging enough. They came out of the corner as two middle-aged people, Qwrk in a dark suit like the salesman, and X in a replica of the dress his female customer was wearing. She had even managed to duplicate the customer's hairstyle, which had been difficult, coloured as it was with unfamiliar chemicals. The woman gave her a strange look and retreated without buying anything. At least it freed the salesman to attend to their wants. His manners, X thought, were now faultless. He seemed pleased with their large order and promised that the store would deliver the things to Renmark Street that afternoon.

'There's certainly not enough currency left to buy a vehicle after paying for all that,' X said on their way home. 'The few notes that are left must be guarded until Mother finds a job. However, to celebrate the success of our first shopping venture, I'll let you have one of these little silver coins to buy something for yourself.'

Qwrk bought something called bubblegum, which had instructions on its wrapper. He blew large floppy bubbles all the way down the street to their house. X noticed that people seemed to be staring, and hurriedly consulted the PIC.

'Bubblegum is bought and used only by children,' she said. 'And you're still wearing wrinkles and eye-glasses. Quick, change back before Mother sees us.' Mother, she knew, disapproved strongly of simulated-age procedures, ever since Dovis had once turned herself into a clone of Mrs Gombaldu, and Mother, unsuspecting, had talked to her in some detail about what went on at her Wear factory annual party.

21

X checked that the food purchases had been delivered, then went about the house inspecting the new colour schemes. It was amazing what Mother had achieved, using only two mini-tubes of colour concentrate which had been in her handbag on the raft. Mother had rather flamboyant tastes, but X couldn't find it in her heart to comment unfavourably on the inverted-spectrum curtains in the main room, or the wall mural. Mother, was, after all, doing her best to create a home in this alien environment. She was so proud of the mural, which glittered and danced, reflecting and shedding light incessantly.

The furniture delivery people stared at it when they arrived. They stared at Mother, too, for she absently addressed them in eighteenth-century French, having spent all that time learning it on the voyage. And they really stared at Dovis. Dovis didn't take any notice of them. She was more interested in abstract, artistic thought forms than in people, anyhow, and was humming the first bars of H73Chok's 'Concerto for Four Cosmic Fliers and Zyrgonthyzer'. H73Chok was her favourite composer. She sat on one of the new chairs by the window. Her hair blazed in magnificence, lit by the sun piercing the inverted-spectrum curtains. And where she'd walked across the floor, X noticed with irritation, tiny white and yellow flowers had blossomed. One of the delivery men was so amazed that he dropped a table on his foot. Dovis gazed at him, her eyes as luminous and enchanting as stars, and he dropped a chair on his other foot.

'No one ever stares at me,' X thought.

She sometimes had fits of jealousy where Dovis was concerned. 'Never mind, X,' Mother would say to comfort her. 'We can't all be born to beauty. Besides, you have your own special gifts. Your talent for Organizing, unusual in one your age; your dependability; your resourcefulness. It's no wonder you topped the list and won that Organizing scholarship. This family relies upon you utterly. And besides, you have excellent teeth.'

'It relies upon me so utterly,' X thought, 'that on my birthdays I'm never given lovely exotic presents like the ones they give to Dovis; fabulous jewels and silver hairsnoods.' She tried to remember her last birthday gifts. 'A laundry robot,' she thought glumly, 'and a household-accounts file.'

Her talent for resourcefulness was tested after the furniture-store people left. Father wouldn't help. He was still engrossed in the gambling section of the newspaper, and X suspected that he was working out a system to beat the local one. Qwrk just shoved a pink and white ruffled bed into the room that was going to be his, then shut the door and sealed it all round with some invisible substance he'd invented. X guessed that he'd materialized more of his lab equipment from the space raft, even though she'd forbidden it. Dovis was levitating dreamily up among the light fittings and wouldn't come down. Mother helped, but was maddening. She kept bewailing the beautiful, lightweight household equipment left behind on Zyrgon. 'Supposing the Government confiscates all our goods when they find out your father's skipped off?' she said forlornly.

'You're forgetting Lox,' X said, so infatuated by that name that she repeated it. 'Lox promised he'd conceal everything in an air pocket.'

'I don't think I can bear this exile.'

'It may not be for as long as we think. Lox knows some

23

very influential people. At any moment he could beam us saying, "Come home, all is forgiven". Meanwhile this is our home now, and we must make the best of it. I'm going to show Father how to prepare a local meal.'

It was difficult to make Father come out from behind the newspaper, but X pushed him into the kitchen and opened the recipe book at the first entry. 'I'll help you this first time, but after that you must work things out alone,' she said. 'So you'd better pay attention.'

Father, with sparse enthusiasm, followed the strange recipe and under her supervision assembled the basic ingredients into a whole. He placed the container into the oven and watched the cooking process through its glass-panelled door. He stopped sulking and became mildly interested in the way the oven worked by transmitting heat to the container.

'But how do I remove the dish at the stated time?' he asked.

'With things called oven mitts or oven cloths,' X explained. 'As we have neither, you must make do with this piece of discarded material from Mother's curtains. There's no problem that can't be solved somehow.' She placed a bowl of fruit in the centre of the new table, then summoned the family for the meal. Father proudly presented the food he'd cooked.

'It's called Apple Charlotte,' X said. 'I know it looks and smells quite different from envelope food, but it's Father's first attempt, so no tactless comments from any of you.' The Apple Charlotte, however, was delicious, and everyone had several helpings.

'Their food is much nicer than I thought,' Mother said, pleased. 'And certainly more attractive visually than transparent party food.'

'Or envelopes,' Dovis said. She tried one of the yellow crescents from the bowl of unfamiliar fruits, but couldn't bite easily through its outer layer.

'Its title is banana,' Father said. 'The covering has to be removed before eating. I read about them in the recipe book while I was waiting for the meal to cook. That book is very interesting. For tomorrow's meal I might make a thing called banana cake with lemon glacé icing.'

'Enough of that now,' X said. 'While we're all here together, I'm calling a Family Council to discuss certain important items. The most important is names. Nothing was decided on the voyage, because you all fought and bickered so much over that list in the PIC. So I've selected a few from the thousands you underlined and now you must all choose one name and stick to it.'

It was obvious that their own would sound out of place. Lox had already explained that nobody here was ever called X unless they were a government secret official. And that nobody was called Qwrk at all. During the voyage X had let everyone have a turn with the list, but it hadn't proved a good method. Mother kept choosing names, then discovering others she liked even more, and they'd all been of French extraction, so stubborn was she about the Versailles landing. And then she'd grown sad at the thought of not being able to use her own name in exile, and had refused to have anything more to do with the list.

Dovis had concentrated for all of five seconds, became bored, and had gone away to a corner of the raft to dance. Father had been his usual irritatingly breezy self. 'Later, X,' he'd said. He'd found an old cobwebbed scanner in the chart box of the raft and was trying to locate his star sign through a porthole.

X eyed them sternly now, over the empty Apple Charlotte dish. 'Let's begin,' she said. 'Our family name is Jackson, as you know. Father, you'd better keep Mortimer as your first name, as you've already used it to sign the lease for this house.'

'All right,' he said. 'I don't mind what I'm called. I've spent a lifetime giving false names to various people and organizations.' X saw that he'd just made a bet with Qwrk about how many grains there were in a jar of some odd-looking things called hundreds and thousands bought at the food store. She saw also that he was cheating.

'Stop that and concentrate,' she said, taking the solar reckoner away from him. 'You have to know your name properly, at all times. People will think it very odd if you don't. Right, what is it?'

'Edna?' he asked guiltily. 'Malcolm? Hepzibah?'

X made him write it out a hundred times. She grabbed Dovis by an ankle and tugged her sharply down from the ceiling.

'Astrella, Philome, Fabriola,
Diamanta, Clematis, Gloriola,
Chicquita, Cadance, Albertine,
Cleopatra, Desdemona, Bernardine,
Euphrasia, Ingeborg . . .' Dovis began.

'NO!' said X. 'Lox explained that some people down here become completely carried away when they name their children, but it would be a mistake for us to draw attention to ourselves with unusual names. I've chosen a simple, unadorned one for you instead. Agnes.'

Tears stole softly into Dovis's eyes, like dew-beaded petals. She wept without making one sound, all her poetry quenched.

'If you hate the name of Agnes so much, all right, then!'

X said exasperated. 'You really are the most annoying person! I'll go through the list and cross out the ones you definitely are NOT allowed to have, but I'll leave in some fancy ones. But certainly not Astrella.

'Why not?' asked Qwrk. 'She's so beautiful that people are going to stare at her, anyhow. Even if you make her be called Agnes. Besides, she won't be able to remember a new name for very long. It's taken her fourteen solar years to learn to answer to Dovis. So it doesn't matter what she chooses. Why not let her be Astrella?'

X grudgingly gave in, cutting short Dovis's sonnet of praise and thanksgiving. 'Now there's you,' she said to Qwrk, and inspected some of the names he'd underlined on the voyage.The meanings were printed next to each name. Qwrk had underlined: 'Rowan – famous; Hubbard – intellectual; Lindo – handsome; Obert – illustrious; Lewton – man of refinement.'

'I'll leave you to make the final choice,' he said smugly.

'That's fortunate,' X said crushingly. 'George. George Jackson, and don't argue about it. I'm in charge of this family.'

Mother was the most difficult of all, as she still had her heart set on a French name. 'I'll have elegant writing paper with a monogram made up,' she said. 'I could write a letter to Mrs Gombaldu, and Dovis – I mean Astrella – could kinetize it home.'

'No one must know our whereabouts, Mother. You aren't to contact any of those gabby members of the Fifth-Day Luncheon Club at all. However, I don't suppose it will hurt to let you call yourself Renée while we're down here.' X, tired of haggling over name selections, could hardly be bothered spending time on one for herself.

Her eye fell on page one of the cooking manual. Apple Charlotte.

'Charlotte is also a female name,' she said thankfully. 'It's here in the list. That's what I'll be known as while we're in exile.'

She read aloud a schedule of things the Jackson family — Mortimer, Renée, Astrella, Charlotte and George — had to do in order to live safely in Renmark Street without attracting undue notice. '1. Mother to get a salaried job to renew the currency; 2. Father not to get involved in any gambling situations; 3. Astrella to be discreet about flying, and to do it within the house only, also to desist from reciting her terrible poetry aloud; 4. Qwrk not to mention Knowledge Bank to anyone; 5. Prepare a plausible family history which they must all memorize.'

'Is that all?' asked Mother.

'No,' X said. 'There's something called school. Dovis, Qwrk and I have to go to a school while we're living down here. It's the law.'

THREE

Father arose suspiciously early the next morning and said he was going for a walk. But when he returned, he was driving a gleaming new vehicle.

'A surprise, X,' he said, looking pleased with himself. 'And I didn't steal it, either. I paid for it.'

'But we didn't have enough money left!'

'We have now,' Father said, and placed a great stack of money on the table. The notes had a clever patina of age and usage.

'Did you make them while we were asleep?' Qwrk asked, impressed. 'You're getting much better at it. These are superior to anything you ran up on Zyrgon; exact replicas, and no one could detect otherwise.'

'Mortimer Jackson, I can't turn my back on you for one moment!' X raged. 'You must have the shortest memory in the whole galaxy! Last time you set about making illicit currency on Zyrgon, you were up on a charge before the officials!' Thankful for her powers of concentration gained in the organizing course, she wasted no time in zapping the bundle of notes into the deepest air pocket she could find. She sealed it so tightly that not even the Zyrgonese Shuttle Service's top mechanic could have located the opening. 'You musn't ever tamper with their currency system again, Father. You should have realized that they print only a set number of notes. Now there'll be a discrepancy with the false notes you've put into circulation by buying that car. The authorities will surely find out, and perhaps trace the source back to you.'

'But I didn't print false notes,' Father protested. 'I've been trying to get a word in edgewise. They were real ones, AND going to waste now, in that air pocket! What I did was remove them from ordinary circulation by kinetics. I can't possibly remember all the places. There were too many. I just took them from here and there, but not from people who couldn't afford it. Only from wealthy houses and places of brisk trading.'

'Why can't you act honestly, Father? I do my best to be a shining example to you and train you properly ... '

'I know you do, X. I'm very grateful to have an Organizer who topped the examination lists and won the Scholarship. But I've had all those other years of being Organized by Aunt Hecla. Her influence is hard to overcome.'

'You still have the car,' Qwrk consoled him. 'At least for today. X couldn't possibly make another air pocket large enough to get rid of it. She's used up all her daily ration of power.'

'The vehicle will be got rid of tomorrow,' X said. 'Father may use it for today, but only because we need to go out searching for a school. Mother, you needn't come. One adult is quite enough bother to supervise.'

Father was no better at driving here, she thought grimly, than he was back on Zyrgon. He still challenged other drivers at traffic control lights, with subtle eye signals that meant, 'Let us see who can be first, my friend, to take off when the lights change!'

'There's a fine building which has the appearance of a PIC school up on that hill,' Qwrk said. 'Let's drive there and see.' But when they reached the place, X saw at once that the students were much older than Qwrk. He wouldn't listen when she pointed it out, but jumped out of the car and went looking for an administration office. X hurried after him. She saw that she needn't have worried about Mother's eighteenth-century clothes. Many of the students were wearing garments even weirder.

'Listen, Qwrk,' she said, grabbing his arm. 'These people are definitely not in your chronological age group. You mustn't have expectations that might come to nothing. You obviously won't be admitted to a place like this as a student. I think it's called a university, anyhow, not a school.

'Who said anything about being a student?' Qwrk demanded. 'I'm going to apply for a professorial job and salary. Where's the office?'

He wouldn't return to the car, so X applied a secret, third lumbar vertebral pressure-grip which she'd learned from watching Law Enforcers at drill. It wasn't painful, but it was persuasive, and Qwrk swore in Zyrgonese gutter-language all the way back to the car.

'There's no point in berating me,' she said, shoving him into the back seat and slamming the door. 'The PIC says that people of your age aren't allowed to be professors here. They have to attend schools with others of their rightful age group. We should obey their laws without question, because we're guests on this planet.'

'Guests usually arrive by invitation,' Dovis pointed out. 'But we arrived by contraband space-raft.'

'You're not to mention that space-raft to anyone! And I just hope you've memorized the family history which I prepared last night. Any school we apply to is certain to ask questions.'

But it was obvious that Dovis hadn't bothered to learn one word. X had put a great deal of careful thought into the family history. The Jacksons supposedly had lived in a variety of different countries because of their father's career as an engineer. Father had been disappointed at being made into an engineer. If he HAD to work, he said, he'd prefer people to think that he had a more dramatic occupation such as a video stuntsman or a soldier of fortune. But Lox had stressed the importance of being as ordinary as possible in official documents.

X went through the history in the car and made Dovis repeat it, especially the section which stated that she'd studied dance forms in all the countries they had lived in. That was a precaution in case she ever absently indulged in complicated ground exercises.

They spent a substantial part of the day driving about inspecting schools, but Qwrk, in a negative mood, wouldn't even look at them through the car windows. And then, almost despairing, X found an attractive school within walking distance of their house. It was built of soft red brick, on a gently sloping hillside with a fringe of trees and lawn. There were students in the grounds. X looked at all those girls, laughing in the sunlight. Jaded from all her problems, she wished suddenly that she could be like that, too, carefree, not having to worry about supplies of currency or household management or a father wanted by Law Enforcers on a planet far across the sky.

'This looks a suitable place,' she said. 'When we go inside, you must all be well-behaved.' She tidied Qwrk's hair and made him lick off the equations he'd scribbled on the palms of his hands. He always did that when bored. At least she didn't have to tidy Father, who looked, as always, handsome and dapper. She felt secretly proud of having such a handsome father, even though he was too scatty to deserve such a role in anyone's family group.

'Have you an interview with the Principal?' asked a woman at a reception desk just inside the main entrance.

X had no idea that such a thing was needed, but Father smiled his debonair gambler's smile. 'We've just arrived in this town to live,' he said smarmily. I saw your magnificent establishment as we drove past. My children will be broken-hearted if there are no vacancies.' His eyes were as velvety as a hybrid-antelope's. The woman smiled at him warmly, spoke into a little desk communicator and escorted them into the Principal's office. The Principal's name was Miss Brewster. She was awesome. Even Dovis, after one look, put her hands behind her back and stood politely with her feet turned out, as though attending her Cosmic Flier audition.

But Father looked right into Miss Brewster's eyes and smiled, and his smile was like the sun coming out from behind a large, soggy, week-old cloud. So the interview commenced with Miss Brewster charmed into accepting not only Dovis and X at her school, but also Qwrk. She explained that the school took small boys up to the second grade. Qwrk opened his mouth indignantly, but X applied her secret vertebral grip again, and he closed it. Miss Brewster said that they could all start on Monday, that the account for tuition would be sent by mail, and that the uniforms were available from Guthrie's Department Store. Father kissed her hand on the way out. Miss Brewster looked startled, but pleased.

'You mustn't kiss women's hands here,' X said when

they were in the car again. 'That was applicable only if we'd landed in eighteenth-century Versailles.'

'Sometimes hand kissing is expedient,' said Father.

'How much money is left in the safety vest?' X asked when they found the department store. Father handed her the wallet. It was empty, except for a slim little book that hadn't been there before.

'Trust me, X,' he said. 'While I was out this morning, I put the remainder into a very safe place. I only wish now that I'd put the other money I got by kinetics in the same place, before you zapped it into that air pocket. Lox told me about this safe place before we left. It's called a bank and they give you this little record book . . .'

'A cheque account,' X said. 'I read all about it in the PIC. A correct procedure, but this balance figure scarcely warrants it, Father. There's not going to be enough to pay for the special clothes Miss Brewster said we must have.'

'That's nothing to worry about. I can just add a row of zeros.'

'You certainly will not! Cheque accounts are computer-reviewed regularly. People here are much more financially alert than on Zyrgon. But we must have that school clothing. Miss Brewster sounded so definite about it. I don't want us to look different from anyone else on Monday morning.'

'They also have things called Bankcards,' said Father. 'I collected one when I got the cheque book. Buy now, pay later. No different, really, from what I've been doing on Zyrgon.'

'Except that there, you always bought now with no intention whatsoever of paying later,' X said. 'That won't do here.' She decided, however, that the Bankcard could

34

be used safely, because Mother was sure to find a well-paid job soon. Anyhow, they had no choice. Miss Brewster had been formidable.

She found the store department that sold school clothing. Miss Brewster's school required its students to wear navy-blue blazers with emblems adorning the pockets, and caps with the same emblem. There were striped ties and grey skirts; for Qwrk, short trousers of the same dark grey, and a little peaked cap. Because of Mother's Zyrgonese occupation, they were quite used to trying on strange garments, but Dovis turned pale with horror when she saw her reflection in the mirror. Shocked tears spilled from her eyes and made star patterns on the blazer lapel. X gazed uncertainly at her family clad in the school uniforms. They looked, she decided, horribly like Law Enforcer cadets. Even the makeshift clothing she had prepared for landing was more flattering.

'O! How perfectly . . . NASTY!' Dovis whispered. 'I can't . . . I WON'T wear such pitiful things!'

Father looked at her anxiously, for he couldn't bear to see Dovis upset. Beauty such as hers, he thought, should always be shielded from the little vexations of daily living. He started to tell her that of course she need not wear the school clothes if they made her unhappy, and that she didn't even have to attend Miss Brewster's school if she didn't want to. She could stay home all day instead, and dance, levitate, sing and recite poetry.

X put a stop to that immediately. 'You just listen to me, Dovis Astrella Jackson!' she said fiercely. 'We've got to stay on this planet until Lox says it's safe to go back to Zyrgon. And if we don't obey the local laws, and compulsory attendance at school is one of them, it will mean Detention Centre. Except it's called Prison here, and it's

Father who'll be incarcerated, not us. Children are classified as second-rate citizens. So, if you don't conform by wearing those clothes on Monday, ugly as they are . . .' She tried to think of something powerful enough to bludgeon Dovis into obedience. 'I'll put our new music-machine into the deepest, darkest air pocket I can manufacture!'

Dovis loved the new music-machine, which X had bought because it was customary. She hadn't wanted their household to be different. Dovis delighted in the cassettes with their novel scales and patterns, and played them at every available moment. X hadn't heard her humming H73Chok's music ever since she'd bought that music-machine.

Dovis nodded sullenly, and X went to supervise Father's use of the Bankcard. It was fortunate that she did so. He'd gathered a large stack of things not on the school uniform list, from all over the store. There were coloured umbrellas, a set of smart, matching leather luggage, five sunhats, a collection of elaborate electronic games, a bright yellow inflatable plastic dinghy, and five objects in cases which X recognized from her reading of the PIC to be portable typewriters. She made him put everything back, even though the sales assistant looked very disappointed.

'All those items would have to be paid for eventually,' she pointed out as they drove home with the school clothing. 'People down here don't give things away for nothing, and besides, we didn't need any of them. You're extremely acquisitive as well as being dishonest. Both undesirable characteristics.'

'I fully intended to pay for those things when Mother finds a job,' Father said, but X could read through his eyes, as though they were glass panels with his thoughts written on a screen behind. He'd been thinking that there would no doubt be a change of government on Zyrgon soon, and that they could go home quietly with no possible repercussions from Guthrie's Department Store.

'Remember what happened when you tried a similar policy on Aunt Hecla's moon?' she demanded. 'You thought you'd be safe back on Zyrgon. But just cast your thoughts to those baritone debt-collectors who came to our apartment with a loudvoice hailer and embarrassed us all so dreadfully in front of Mrs Gombaldu! A Singing Telenab. This planet's technology isn't so very far behind ours, you know.'

It was late afternoon and apparently the end of the school day, for the streets were filled with students. X watched them with detached curiosity. They seemed carefree and untroubled, chatting to one another at street corners and exchanging complicated farewells. The car stopped at one of the traffic lights and X wound the window down to listen unobtrusively to two girls on the footpath.

'See you tomorrow, Lisa.'

'Ring me up after dinner tonight. Ask your mother if you can come over to my place to sleep for the weekend. We could go to the pool.'

'Or to Guthrie's to look at autumn clothes.'

'Okay, but don't forget to bring your new album. Ask your Mum can you . . .'

Inexplicably, listening to their chatter, X felt wearily old, as old as Aunt Hecla almost. It was strange, because she was obviously a good deal younger than either of those two girls.

FOUR

Dovis hadn't even begun to put on her school uniform. She had winged dancing sandals on her feet instead of the heavy laced shoes decreed by Miss Brewster, and kept bobbing stubbornly up to the ceiling. And Qwrk refused to acknowledge the existence of his school cap. X, in desperation, called Lox on a speak-beam and asked him to give them both a lecture. He wasn't a Space Shuttle captain for nothing. He told Dovis and Qwrk in a terrifying voice that they must behave and co-operate. He threatened to take all their most treasured possessions out of the air pocket on Zyrgon and sell them in the market.

'You wouldn't dare!' Dovis yelled along the beam, too furious to rhyme. 'My autographed copy of H73Chok's first symphony! Lox, if that's missing when we come back, I'll get horribly even with you, just see if I don't!'

'You won't want to come back to Zyrgon if you don't do as X tells you, young lady,' Lox said sternly. 'If she has to beam me again because you're making things hard for her, I'll squash your hopes of a career with the Cosmic Fliers. I'll just tell their Committee that you have a secret phobia about heights.'

'They'd never believe you! I was the best cadet flier in my training class!'

'Then I'll forge a medical treatment report stating that you need hypnosis before you can levitate even to the ceiling. Yes, I know it's dastardly. I don't care. I'm feeling dastardly, being woken up as early as this!'

He detested the morning hours, and dealt smartly with Qwrk, too, by threatening to break into the Knowledge Bank administration office and fix it so that a little subtle bribery be found in Qwrk's professor-nomination forms. Qwrk was so alarmed that he slapped the school cap on his head and stood meekly by the front door.

'Thanks for the assistance, Lox,' X said gratefully. 'I'm sorry for disturbing you at such an hour.'

'If it had been anyone else, I would have let that beam zip away unanswered. How are things with you in general?'

X felt terribly ashamed that she'd had to summon his help about the school uniforms. She wished that she had something splendid to report, such as having received half a dozen betrothal offers since landing, anything to make his interest more than casual.

'Mother is going to look for a job today,' she said. 'And Father's behaving himself reasonably well, though he bought a car without permission and I haven't had time to get rid of it yet. We're all very homesick, but that's natural. Do the authorities believe we've gone to Aunt Hecla's?'

'I think so. They're suspicious, of course, that anyone would want to go there in the ice season, and there's a tremendous commotion at the Law Enforcing Office while they go through your father's lottery files in detail. But apparently they do believe he's just skipped off to the second moon and taken all of you with him to avoid embarrassment. Not to worry. The Government is sure to topple soon. It's been in power for a record three months as it is. You'll be able to come home shortly, I daresay, before anyone finds out you've gone to You Know Where. X, I've got to go. Interrupted sleep does ruinous things to my complexion. Please remember that in future.'

A great yawn echoed along the beam. X said goodbye, and watched the beam slowly fade, feeling mingled sadness and joy at hearing Lox's voice. When the beam faded altogether, it was like being cast adrift on floating space-ice.

She packed a midday meal for three. Father offered to drive them to the new school, but X thought it wiser to avoid any emotional farewell scenes in public. Mother was being quite emotional enough as it was. 'X, look after them,' she implored tearfully. 'Guard them well, and don't let any harm come near them. Defend them with your life, if necessary.'

'Nothing will go amiss,' X said. 'I've already told them how to behave.'

Qwrk and Dovis behaved very well on the way to school. Lox's threats had been effective. Dovis walked demurely, and although her beauty was still startling, even in the stiff uniform clothes, she had the approximate appearance of an ordinary schoolgirl. Qwrk was huffily silent.

'You'll be all right if you don't do anything spectacular,' X warned him. 'You mustn't act differently from any other children of your age level. I know it will be hard, but you must do it well enough to fool the authorities.' She was worried, and the anxiety felt like a tight, migrainic band across her forehead. Qwrk looked at her and softened, for he had a kindly nature underneath his formidable IQ.

'Very well,' he said. 'I'll do my best, in spite of the humiliation.'

Mrs Sharples, the school secretary, showed them to their respective classrooms. She took Qwrk into a room full of very small boys and girls. X saw him blink and gaze incredulously at the miniature chairs and tables, the display boards, counting games and coloured wooden toys, but to her relief, he behaved beautifully. He said good morning blandly to the teacher and sat down cross-legged on the floor amongst the children. He even put his thumb into his mouth.

'What a sweet little boy,' the teacher murmured.

Mrs Sharples took Dovis to another part of the building. Dovis showed alarming signs of drifting away inside her mind. X pinched her sharply and whispered, 'Cosmic Fliers, forged mental-health certificate, phobia of heights.' Dovis came back, glaring. The students in her room were reciting poetry, and she brightened visibly and took the seat shown to her. Everyone stared at her beauty and smiled at her. X reflected enviously that beauty softened life for anyone who possessed it. People enjoyed being close to beauty, like warming their hands at a winter fire. Mere organizing skills seem tepid in comparison. Someone was offering to share a text-book with Dovis, someone else leaned forward to ask her name, even the instructor was gazing at her with indulgent admiration.

'This way, Charlotte,' said Mrs Sharples. 'We've put you in Form 1B. I'm sure you'll like that group of girls very much.'

Form 1B was studying mathematics. Their instructor introduced X briskly. 'This is Charlotte Jackson, who has been living overseas. Charlotte's elder sister and small brother are also enrolled at this school. I hope you

41

will make them all feel welcome.' Everyone looked cautiously at X, not committing themselves. X placed her new materials tidily upon the desk provided and prepared to work as directed. She had no trouble with the mathematics. One couldn't spend five years in a household containing Qwrk and not absorb mathematical formulae as though it were air.

She didn't quite know what to do when she'd completed the work. Nobody else had finished so quickly. She looked around the classroom, which was pleasant, with wide windows overlooking the grounds. Suddenly a little folded slip of paper landed on her desk. X looked at it with surprise. It had 'Dallas' written on it, and she knew that to be a city in the United States of America. She opened the paper curiously and read its message: 'Dallas, Bronwyn didn't really mean it about your new perm. I think it looks great! Bronwyn is always snaky on Monday mornings. If you aren't speaking to her this week, do I have to, too? I want to borrow her pencil-sharpener. RSVP. Michelle.'

X re-read it, puzzled. Someone reached forward and gave her arm an indignant poke. 'That message is for Dallas! Pass it on!'

Dallas, a girl, not a city, apparently the one on X's left, was also looking at her unfavourably. X handed her the slip of paper.

'It's rude to read other people's letters,' whispered the girl behind.

'How was I supposed to know it was a personal letter when it had no envelope or postage stamp?' X asked, not much liking the appearance of that girl. She had a round, silly face, unkind eyes, and obviously a very high opinion of herself.

'Being smart on our first day here, are we?' she said. 'You're a new girl, and you'd better not forget it, either!'

It seemed an obvious statement, which X thought better to ignore. How could one forget that one was a new member of a community? She inspected the other students. The girl on her right-hand side flashed her an unexpected, friendly, charming smile. X's spirits lifted for the first time since the space-raft had landed.

That particular girl was having trouble with the mathematics, despite the smile. The pen she was using ran dry and she rattled the contents of an untidy small box, trying to find another. The teacher said crossly, 'Jenny Roland, I wish you'd bring a spare biro to school! I've told you quite often enough!' Jenny Roland used a ragged pencil instead, chewed at one end like foliage. Then she came to the end of her supply of paper. She searched noisily through her work folder and tore out a page from another section. Her written work was messy. She dropped things, she couldn't find things, and the girls nearby kept giving her irritated looks. But X, who admired order and neatness, found to her surprise that she liked that girl.

Miss Harrow went to the board and wrote down the correct answers to the mathematical problems. None of the other students had them all correct. X had. Miss Harrow came to check her work, but her eyebrows rose sharply. 'Charlotte, why on earth have you used such a strange method to work out these problems?' she asked. 'How did you arrive at this particular answer, for instance? I can't understand your system at all.'

'I divided the lateral by the oblong, then squared it and advanced it to the nearest power of four.'

'Are you being humorous?' Miss Harrow demanded crisply.

'There's nothing humorous about mathematics,' X said, surprised. 'I just followed the correct procedure to arrive at a conclusion. This method is the one I always use.'

'It's certainly not the one we use here. I'll arrange for you to have special remedial work to catch up with the others.'

'But Charlotte got all those problems right, Miss Harrow,' said Jenny Roland. Miss Harrow just frowned at her and returned to the board. X realized that she'd drawn unwanted attention to herself by getting all those answers right. With the next set of problems, she made several deliberate mistakes and worked to Miss Harrow's system, even though it seemed time-wasting and inefficient.

Mathematics was followed by a class in French, taken by a different teacher. X was able to cope, because of Mother studying that language so stubbornly on the voyage, though the teacher said she had a strange accent. Jenny Roland was scolded, because all the pages of her text suddenly fell to the floor like rain-sodden leaves. 'What have you been doing to that book?' the teacher said. 'I hope you realize it's one of a class set, and that you'll have to pay for the replacement. Really, Jenny, now that you're no longer in primary school, I'd hoped for more responsible behaviour.'

'Sorry, Mrs Merril,' said Jenny Roland cheerfully. 'A leg of my bed fell off, and I tried to prop it up with a stack of books and this one was on top. It didn't take the strain. But I'll fix it with sticky-tape.'

One of the pages had landed on X's shoe. The margins were filled with scribbled pictures of horses, one of which looked a bit like a hybrid-antelope. X felt a treacherous jab of homesickness, so intense that she lost concentration. She couldn't find the place when asked to read aloud, and was told that she must pay attention, even if she was new.

'Too busy reading other people's letters,' the girl behind hissed nastily in her ear.

X was glad when they were allowed outside for recess. She looked hurriedly for Dovis and Qwrk. Qwrk was heading swiftly through the school gate, but she hauled him back inside. 'What happened?' she demanded.

'Appalling things! That woman made me cut coloured paper into primitive shapes and as though that wasn't insulting enough, she told me what the shapes were called! Circle, rectangle, square . . . Then she read a book aloud to the group, a ridiculous, biologically impossible story about ducklings! What a way to teach people, telling them lies! And they sang inane songs, with actions to match the words. They made me be a banana!'

'But Qwrk, we calculated last night what to expect.'

'The PIC didn't mention that a beastly little girl called Melissa would pick me up and carry me about the room! She said I was her little friend. That teacher found it amusing when I lodged an official complaint. They don't mind at all about infringing people's personal territorial zones! Mine was infringed so many times that I lost count. Even by the instructor. She kept stroking my hair and telling me that I'd love that class when I got over feeling new. X, you wouldn't believe it, but they count on wooden beads threaded to a wire frame! And only up to ten!'

'It's just the way they do things here,' X said. 'You could have got on with your private mental research while you did those simple little tasks.'

'I'm going home!'

'No, you're not!'

His classmates were playing in a fenced section filled with outdoor equipment. There was a metal ramp which they slid down, squealing, but X couldn't understand their excitement. Gravity was just gravity. There was also a wooden frame filled with sand, in which some of them were digging.

'Go over and join them, Qwrk,' X ordered. 'Take your mind off things by working out the metallurgic stresses in that sliding ramp. And if you dare go home before the correct departure time, I'll contact Lox again. Just think how it will look in the *Zyrgon Morning Star*, a huge headline saying, 'Newest Knowledge Bank Professor Accused of Bribing His Way In'. Such things go on, of course, but everyone pretends they don't, so your name will still be disgraced. Mother wouldn't be able to lift her head at Fifth-Day Luncheons.'

Qwrk gave her a fiercely mutinous look, but plodded across to the sandpit, defeated. X went to make sure that Dovis was staying out of trouble. She was dancing, but not, X was relieved to see, levitating. A group of fascinated girls watched. 'Those steps are terrific, Astrella!' one of them said. 'Did you learn them in America?'

Dovis just smiled mysteriously and avoided speech. She had no real need to talk, anyhow, for the girls clustered about her were making enough noise, exclaiming about her grace, her wondrous hair, her skin, her beauty.

X turned away and approached the girls of her own class. The Dallas one said, 'What do you mean, opening a note addressed to me? You've got a nerve!'

'Everyone has,' X said patiently. 'Thousands of them.'

'I told you she was a smarty,' said the one with the round face. 'If there's one thing I can't stand, it's new girls who carry on as though they own the whole school.'

'Leave her alone, Michelle,' said Jenny Roland. 'Don't be so mean to her on her first day. Remember how you felt.'

'I got along okay on my first day,' Michelle said disagreeably. 'That's because I didn't show off and read other people's personal letters.'

They all turned their backs, except Jenny Roland. 'Have you really been all over the world, like Miss Harrow said?' she asked. 'I've never been anywhere, except to Crescent Bay for holidays, and that was only staying in a crummy caravan. It was murder.'

X stared at her, aghast. The PIC data on murder had horrified her.

'Oh, it wasn't all that bad,' Jenny said, surprised by her reaction. 'I'm exaggerating. But it's pretty grim going on holidays with my family. I always have to share the tent annexe with Shane and Andrew and they fight every minute. How old is your little brother?'

'George is five,' X said. 'And that's my sister Astrella over there.'

'I know. Michelle pointed her out and said she was your sister. She's gorgeous!'

'It has disadvantages. Once when my family was on holiday in the Space Shut . . . I mean, while we were travelling, the other passengers all fought amongst themselves for the privilege of sitting next to Astrella and holding her hand. Even the pilot. There was almost a riot. The raft steward had to make Astrella sit all by herself in the luggage compartment.'

'A raft?' said Jenny. 'How super! Did you really go for a holiday on a raft?'

'I didn't really mean a raft, I meant an ordinary jet plane,' X said, cross with herself for prattling little family anecdotes to the first friendly face.

After morning recess, her class changed into short green skirts and played netball. X didn't know the rules, but to her surprise, she was quite adept. She had good reflexes, developed through years of forestalling Dovis from becoming airborne in unsuitable places.

At the end of the session, one of the girls said grudgingly, 'For a new drip from overseas, you might even make it into the netball team. Not many people can score five goals in a row. I guess you can't help having a dreggy name like Charlotte, either.'

'What's wrong with the name Charlotte?' X said. 'I chose it myself . . . er, I was named for an esteemed ancestor.'

'You talk crazy!' said Michelle.

X decided that she'd better not talk at all, nor volunteer any information during lunch recess. The food she'd packed didn't look different from the other students' lunches. The PIC has been quite explicit about the art of making sandwiches. She sat near the girls of her class, but not with them, where she could overlook Qwrk's section of the playground. A small girl had one arm twisted about his neck and was feeding him grapes one by one, as though he were a fledgling bird. Qwrk seemed resigned, and X could tell that he was engaged in private mental research, so she didn't worry about him.

Dovis was the nucleus of a circle of girls, who were arranging her hair into different styles, all squabbling to have a turn. X watched tensely, prepared to cover up any astonishing remark or action, but it was apparent that Dovis had somehow managed to merge into the ways of that group in a very short space of time. X's supervision wasn't really needed, but she fretted and worried, from habit, all through the rest of the long afternoon in the classroom.

At its end she collected Qwrk and made him put on his little peaked cap. He was so elated to be free of Melissa's attentions that he was supercharged, like an ice-season emergency battery. She held his hand firmly while they waited for Dovis by the front entrance. Jenny Roland sped past and called over her shoulder, 'See you tomorrow, Charlotte!' in a breathless rush. She ran down the driveway, things spilling from her bag. She almost had a collision with a car belonging to a teacher, who leaned out the window and rebuked her. X wondered idly how that girl had managed to reach her age unscathed. She was the most disorganized person X had ever met.

Dovis emerged from school with her hair in two ornate braids. 'Created by a person called Sally Webster who is also bringing me some beige eyeshadow tomorrow,' she said happily. 'And Lynne is inviting me to her house one evening. I was very much admired at this school. It wasn't as hateful as I thought it would be, and nobody noticed these horrible clothes, because they all wore the same. I might even consider going back there tomorrow, if only to receive my gift of beige eyeshadow. Imagine, beige, such a romantic colour! So different from those boring gold eyelid decorations on Zyrgon that everyone wears, even Law Enforcers.'

'While we're living on this planet, you'll be going to school every day, except for a two-day break at the end of each week.'

'People don't have to attend school if they develop illness,' Qwrk said. 'Melissa said she missed two weeks when she had her appendix removed. If I can't tolerate it at any time, that's what I'll do. Remove my appendix.'

'I utterly forbid you to do any such thing!' X said, but knowing the day-long ordeal he'd borne, and pleased with Dovis for coping so successfully, she stopped at a corner shop and bought three of the coloured frozen things on sticks that other students were buying. She knew it was a frivolous waste of money, which they couldn't really afford, but those things were unknown on Zyrgon, and she'd been curious ever since she'd read about them in the PIC.

FIVE

When they got home, the house was empty.

'Where are they?' Dovis demanded tearfully. 'I shall tell you! The Zyrgonese Law Enforcers must have traced us, and come all the way down here to arrest poor Father. And Mother refused to be parted from him, so they dragged her back, too, wailing and lamenting, as well as confiscating the space-raft. We're marooned!'

'Then I can leave that ridiculous school and be the salary-earner,' Qwrk said, pleased.

'There's sure to be some simple explanation. Perhaps they've left a message.' X checked the kitchen table where Father kept a pad and pencil to list his daily food shopping, and useful hints gathered from the television set. She read swiftly down the untidy list: 'Grain cereal that snaps, crackles and pops; solution to clean dishes – television said that Brighto is best – one large bottle of Brighto; query, what is a WhizzVid Mini Home Entertainment Centre? Television says no household complete without one 874 6666 four lines ring for easy terms. PIC vague on subject.'

There were many similar notes, but nothing explaining their parents' absence. The car was also missing. Dovis looked scared and retreated a long way into her mind.

'Don't worry, X,' Qwrk said. 'If the worst has come to

the worst, and the Law Enforcers have confiscated the raft, Lox can beam us back.'

'He couldn't. A transport beam needs an operator on either end. Lox and I could beam you and Dovis back, of course, but then I'd still be marooned. You academics don't know anything!'

'I think I know enough to make us another raft. It might take a little time, naturally, to work out the calculations . . .'

'The PIC deals with this planet's technology only, and besides, what would you use for fuel? I'm sure there's no need for concern. Mother is probably still looking for a job.'

'But she said that nothing would prevent her being here to welcome us home from school. She said it many times, very emotionally. Perhaps something went wrong. She might have said something incriminating at her job interview, and they arrested her for being an alien. And Father refused to be parted from her. Same state of affairs, different Detention Centre.'

'Qwrk, put the kettle on,' X said. She was beginning to find it a comforting custom, this putting the kettle on and making the drink they called tea. During a crisis, that's what one did. It was in all their books, on all their video entertainment programmes. The fragrance of the tea when she poured it was alluring enough to draw Dovis back from her time-out.

'First little crisis and you retire,' X scoffed.

'I wouldn't call two missing parents a little crisis,' Qwrk said. 'And we have no one to turn to here, no Aunt Hecla, no Mrs Gombaldu – bore though she is – no Lox. Also, no currency left, and on top of all that, I have to do something called homework for that unbelievable school. A list of ten things starting with the letter A.'

'Arliddian,' said Dovis.

'Arliddian?'

'Oh, Qwrk, you remember when we went to the opening of the underwater cavern, and they had that marvellous octet with the coloured music. That was the name of the octet, Arliddian.'

'Qwrk can't possibly put that on his list. He has to put down things that everyone in his class will recognize. Apple. Simple things like that.'

Qwrk wrote down 'apple' and lazily pretended that he couldn't think of anything else.

'Don't expect me to do that task for you,' X said crossly. She didn't add milk to her tea. The PIC claimed that strong black tea was a most powerful remedy for worry, but before she could test it, Mother walked in.

'I've found a wonderful job!' she cried ecstatically. 'I'm now a Designer at a place which has its own boutique!'

'What's a boutique? It sounds French and I just hope you haven't been experimenting with time travel and slipping back to Versailles when I told you not to.'

'Oh, X, it's nothing like that. This morning after you left, all looking so hideous, I designed and made three garments, then I went out and searched for the most elegant Wear Design place in town. The manager was so impressed she offered me a job starting tomorrow. That boutique is charming! I won't even have to process my designs from now on, just create them on paper. They have people in a special workroom who do all the tedious work. And oh, I've been paid a huge sum of currency for those three garments! All I have to do is take this slip of paper to the bank and they'll give me lots of money in exchange. And at the end of every week, I shall be paid a huge salary! Is that tea you've made, X? I'd love some,

53

though I've discovered that it's smarter to drink a thing called coffee. That's what they gave me at the boutique during the job interview. It tasted nasty, but apparently it's smart to drink it. Oh, I should say that I'm sorry to be late. I didn't notice how the time rushed by while I was chatting to that manager.'

'Where's Father?'

'I let him have the day off. Poor darling, he hasn't had much fun since we arrived, getting you all settled into that school and buying a car and everything. He said he was going out to find a Zoomtrack, only it's so strange here, X, they use animals instead of sleds. People sit on them and the one who reaches a stipulated line first wins. Father explained it all to me. He made a study of it by watching the television set.'

'I was the one who got us settled into house and school and everything!' X said indignantly. 'I'm the Organizer and as I'd forbidden Father to go gambling, you had no right to give him permission!'

'Don't frown like that, X. You'll end up as plain as Mrs Gombaldu's Mabla, and who would want to look like her? Now, I haven't yet asked Qwrk and Dovis about school. Was it too terrible, Qwrk?'

Qwrk launched into a passionate tirade against wooden counting-frames, homework, play areas filled with sand, singing games and little girls called Melissa.

'But I quite liked it there,' Dovis interrupted. 'Everyone was gracious to me. They aren't nearly as spiteful as those girls in CF Audition Training. If we have to be exiled on this planet, I suppose that Miss Brewster's school is as good a place as any to pass the time.'

'Mother, you didn't ask how MY day was,' X said, battling unusual resentment.

'But your days are always so totally boring . . . I mean competent,' Mother said, surprised.

'All the same, I would like to be asked.'

'Well then, X, how was your day?' Mother asked, sounding, X thought, just like Aunt Hecla calming an antelope.

'I managed very well. I always do.'

'There, I told you so!' said Mother, and went away to do exotic things to her hair in preparation for her glamorous new job. Dovis began limbering exercises in the main room and X knew that it wouldn't be any use speaking to her for hours. Qwrk sat at the table scowling at the A list.

'You can't stay there,' X said disagreeably. 'I'll have to attend to the evening meal, seeing that Father isn't here to do his rightful job.'

She opened the cooking book and read one of the recipes, making no sense of it. She was too concerned about Father and the unknown, possibly dangerous Zoomtrack. The cup of black tea was now cold, but before she could replenish it, Father strolled in, whistling blithely. The others came running to greet him. He showered money over the table.

'I won it all from gambling, X, I'm sorry to say. It was so easy, though I must admit I probably have more flair than most people. It's not so different from Zyrgon. A similar system, in many ways, even to the betting odds. But I assure you that I didn't try to bribe anyone. It wasn't necessary. I just used Qwrk's solar reckoner.'

'Using that reckoner for gambling was illegal even on Zyrgon Zoomtrack, as you very well know!'

'Nobody saw me. I regard that solar reckoner as a trifling little adjunct, anyhow, and very useful, too, being able to calculate times of arrival with no margin of error. I wonder that the people down here haven't thought of something like it before. They use such haphazard methods. In the main event of the day, everyone was placing bets on animal number eight, but the reckoner indicated clearly that number four would win, in a time of two minutes thirty-five seconds.'

'It's not ethical,' X protested. 'We're visitors here, and it's not at all fair to use advanced technological equipment to amass money. I should make you take it all back.'

'I can't,' Father said smugly. 'The track has closed for the night. I really did like that place. I think I'll try to talk Aunt Hecla into starting a similar establishment on Zyrgon. Those hybrids of hers could easily be trained to race in a straight line. I might even be able to sell some shares while I'm down here, a sort of inter-galactic syndicate.'

'I'll have none of that!' X said. 'It was that syndicate crowd at the Zyrgonese Zoomtrack who got you into trouble in the first place! I don't want you mixing with similar people here. From now on, gambling places are strictly out of bounds for you. Oh, it's so hard to bring you up nicely! You're to remain in the house and devote yourself to household tasks, apart from legitimate errands such as buying food. And put that pile of money away where I don't have to look at it and feel irritated. We don't even need it now. Mother has a well-paid job.'

Mother told him about the boutique. 'They loved my designs,' she said. 'They'd never seen anything quite like them before. Of course, having them already made up for display helped. Design number one was gold tissue, cut rather like the garment I made for Mrs Gombaldu to celebrate the end of last ice-season. And design number two was pearlrock synthetic with fire-tongue lapping, most spectacular. And number three . . .'

'Mother! Just WHERE did you get the fabrics to make those garments?'

'Oh, X, don't nag! I had to have proper working materials.'

'We didn't have Wear fabrics aboard the space-raft. You must have asked Dovis to kinetize them from that warehouse in downtown Zyrgon! It was the only way you could have got them. You certainly couldn't have bought pearlrock synthetic and fire-tongue lapping locally. I've explained a thousand times, no matter how nostalgic we feel, no matter how dire the need, NOTHING is to be removed by kinetics from Zyrgon at all! No wonder those people in the shop . . .'

'Boutique, dear.'

'. . . were impressed by the novelty of your designs.'

Mother's eyes flickered guiltily to one of the wall cupboards. X flung open its doors. There was a large roll of cobwebby hummingspider lace, woven hybrid cloth, reels of transparent thread and rare butterfly-orchid garment studs, and a swathe of delicate crystal net, which was processed to change colour at the wearer's slightest movement.

'You can't use any of this,' X said. 'You'll just have to make do with the local products. Dovis, you must kinetize all this back to Zyrgon.'

'But I don't see why I can't use the Wear ingredients I'm accustomed to! It's not hurting anyone! I cut my very first garment out of pearlrock synthetic. It was for Lox, when he entered for the Mr Galaxy competition. Oh, it's not fair!'

'A bit of hummingspider lace won't cause any

inconvenience,' Father began. Dovis took Mother's hand and held it tenderly. Mother manufactured tears like jewels and sent them cascading down her cheeks. Qwrk eyed X belligerently, for he hated to see Mother cry.

'If you don't behave yourselves this instance, I'll send you all to your rooms without any supper,' X said icily.

'Missing supper won't be any privation,' Qwrk said. 'There doesn't happen to be any. All you did was stare at the cooking book and mutter.'

'Father is supposed to prepare the meals! Refer any complaints to him. I certainly didn't give him permission to be out gadding and gambling instead of staying home properly to arrange nutrition for this household. It seems to me that I'm expected to attend to everything! The Organizing, the meal preparations . . .'

'But . . .' said Father.

'Silence! I won't have you answering me back! It was difficult enough organizing this family back on Zyrgon. None of you realize how hard, how exhausting . . . And Qwrk isn't the only one who has to do extra work for school in his leisure hours . . . Oh, I've got a good mind to RESIGN!' X's voice blurred and stumbled to a stop. She couldn't manage to get any more words out, because she was afraid that each one would be awash with tears.

Everyone stared.

'X, it's quite alarming to hear you speak like this!' said Mother.

'She didn't mean it,' Dovis said nervously. 'Did you, X? You can't say things like that. It could very well give us a feeling of insecurity, and after all, you're supposed to maintain a stable family atmosphere for us to develop our talents.'

'Her voice has never been so emotional,' Qwrk said

with interest. 'Shall I use my solar reckoner to research the causes?'

'Perhaps it's emotion caused by hunger,' Father said. 'And I have a cure for that. Before I went out today, I created a superb meal called Chicken Kiev. It's in the oven now, just waiting to be reheated. You'll feel much better, X, after you've tasted my Chicken Kiev.'

'Even so, such deviations from X's usual psychological behaviour should be analysed.'

'Don't you dare analyse me!' X said. 'Show some respect. And Mother, stop offering me that ridiculous handkerchief. I wasn't about to weep. I never do. Household Organizers never cry or give way to weakness. It was just emotional hunger, as Father said.'

←━━━━━━━━━━━━━━━━━━━━━━━━━━━━━

SIX

'Did you finish that homework list?' X asked on the way to school.

'Yes, I've decided to deal philosophically with the school situation from now on,' Qwrk said, but he looked doleful. X remembered how he'd always dashed gaily off to Knowledge Bank, and it tugged at her heart to watch his dragging footsteps.

'Listen, Qwrk,' she said to console him. 'After school I'll beam Lox and get another report on what's happening.'

'We should have spent this exile in the air pocket with our belongings. Much simpler.'

'Less safe. Too many people hide like that from the Enforcers. They've developed highly accurate person-detectors now. Think of the humiliation of being dragged out with everyone from the apartment-block watching.'

'Then we should have gone to Aunt Hecla's moon.'

'Mother wouldn't have spent an exile there. You know how she hates quicksnow and gales and the smell of prairie grass. This, believe me, was the only alternative. There's your little friend waiting for you at the gate.'

Qwrk nobly allowed himself to be picked up and carried to the sandpit. As soon as Dovis set foot in the school grounds, she was surrounded by the admiring girls of yesterday.

'What shampoo do you use, Astrella? Oh, your hair's so shiny!'

'Astrella, sit next to me for French! Oh, I wish I looked like you!'

'Astrella, sit next to me for English. For music. For everything!'

X went to her own classroom, where there was no welcoming committee, but instead, a small handwritten notice taped to her desk: *Weirdies sit here*. She didn't know what a weirdie was, but it was obviously meant as an insult, for Michelle Hudson was smirking unpleasantly in the seat behind.

'What's a weirdie?' X asked, seeking information.

'You're one. We never had such a nutcase as you in this class before.'

X was tempted to zap Michelle into her own personal air pocket for ever, but instead sat down with dignity and gave her attention to the first lesson. It was called Consumer Education, and the teacher asked for examples of the pitfalls of buying goods.

Dallas told how she'd bought a tube of mascara which had a label claiming that it wouldn't run in the rain, but it did. She treated it as though she'd been criminally robbed, and that it was a case for investigation by the highest Law Enforcer on the planet, X thought.

'Charlotte Jackson,' the teacher said. 'Your turn.'

X could have given plenty of Zyrgonese examples, from various deals her father had made with naïve people. 'Houses,' she said instead. 'When inspecting a house, it's wise to ignore the salesperson and make your own assessment. All salespeople speak with tongues of silver, calculated only to distract. With houses, you should inspect carefully for rising damp, which is difficult to eradicate afterwards. I rented . . . my family rented a house in Renmark Street, and we're only now discovering its hidden defects. Faulty timber has been used for the window frames, and the builder failed to research time and motion. The workbench heights are inconvenient as a result. The main room ceiling shows signs of cracking, and it isn't Dovis's fault . . . I mean, all these things are examples of how prospective customers must be wary of pitfalls.' She sat down.

Miss Chandler looked impressed and said that it was a pleasant change to find someone in the class who took such a thorough interest in the subject.

Michelle leaned forward and tweaked X's hair. 'Boy, are you weird!' she hissed.

'I am not a boy,' X whispered back. 'My hair is short for efficiency. And don't pull it like that again!'

During Mathematics, Mrs Sharples came with a message that the headmistress wished to speak to Charlotte Jackson.

'Astrella? George? Has anything happened to them?' X asked nervously out in the corridor.

'Of course not, dear. There's no need to look so worried. It's just that we tried to contact your home about a little matter, but no one answered the telephone. And Astrella said that you always handle any queries at new schools. Miss Brewster would like to see you for a few minutes, that's all.'

Qwrk's homework list was on the desk in the office.

'Did George really do this work by himself, Charlotte?' Miss Brewster asked.

'Yes, I gave him one example to start the list, but no

more,' X said. 'Hasn't he completed it? On the way to school he told me he had.'

'He's completed it,' Miss Brewster said and held out the list.

X read the ten things starting with the letter A: 'Aragonite. Apogeotropism. Azygous. Argon Laserphotocoagulator. Autoxidation. Antonomasia. Astatic Galvanometer. Arbitration Court. Autochthonism.'

'Oh,' she said.

'Not only did he spell all those words correctly, but he knew, when questioned, what every one of them meant,' said Miss Brewster. 'Has your little brother ever had an intelligence test, Charlotte?'

'Not recently,' X said warily.

'We think he should. Miss Delaney, George's teacher, thought yesterday that he was just shy, because of being new to the school. He didn't answer any questions put to him or communicate with the other children. But there is obviously more to George than meets the eye. Has he shown any precocity at home?'

X thought of the Zyrgonese apartment, where the walls sprouted intricate rock crystals, grown by Qwrk; his laboratory which took up the entire top floor; the senior students who arrived to consult him about physics and astronomy, and the lucrative income he'd had from the age of three working out financial horoscopes for business people.

'George has never shown more than standard intelligence,' she lied.

'That's very strange. Miss Delaney and I believe that it would be a waste of George's time and abilities if he remained in the prep grade. We must arrange for him to work at a higher level. When would it be convenient for your parents to come to school to discuss it?'

'Mother's just started a new job. I don't think she could ask for time off. And Father's fully occupied, too.' X had left him at home with strict instructions to devote himself to household duty. She'd also forbidden him to answer the telephone, knowing how much he liked to chat to anybody, even total strangers.

Miss Brewster wasn't satisfied. She was delighted to have found a potential genius in her school, and meant to make the most of it. 'At this school, we believe in developing each child's capabilities,' she said rather frostily. 'Even if your parents do not appear to be interested, please take them this letter and ask them to contact me, Charlotte. Thank you. You may go back to class.'

At lunch recess X drew Dovis away from her admiring audience to a corner of the playground. 'The administrator of this school has become suspicious about Qwrk,' she said.

'Mmm? What did you say, X?' Dovis asked vaguely. She was contemplating the school garden, bright with seasonal flowers.

'Listen, Dovis! They've discovered that Qwrk knows a bit more than two and two make four. What am I to do?'

'The boisterous kiss of life

Given to the earth

By burgeoning summer,' Dovis murmured.

'Joyous the summer's fair lips

Upon the withered hands of winter trees . . .'

'It's useless trying to discuss things with you!' X said. 'Just one problem after another, which I have to solve! Dovis, I wish that you'd sometimes try to help . . .'

Two of Dovis's class members approached, one

carrying a can of soft drink bought at the school kiosk, another bearing a bun. Dovis took both as a matter of course, with only a melting smile as payment. She was quite used to people bringing her gifts.

'Sit next to me for lunch, Astrella!'

'No, sit next to ME! You sat next to Fiona yesterday. It's my turn.'

X went drearily over to her group and sat on the sun-warmed grass to eat her lunch. Although she sat close to the girls, she didn't feel a part of the group. Occasionally one would half turn to include her politely in the general conversation, but it didn't happen very often. She told herself proudly that she preferred to be left alone. There were too many traps in conversation. She ate her lunch without enthusiasm, disliking the strange substance which contained the protein filling. Michelle Hudson giggled.

'Do you always eat the filling of your sandwiches and just throw the bread away?' she asked guilelessly, but her eyes contained pin-points of malice. 'Is it a Peruvian custom?'

'I wasn't living in Peru long enough to adopt any of their customs,' X said haughtily. She watched Dovis get up and wander about among Miss Brewster's flowerbeds, no doubt composing sonnets. Michelle watched her, too.

'Your sister's very pretty,' someone said.

'Pretty, but weird,' said Michelle. 'You're all peculiar in your family.'

'We're quite an ordinary family,' X said, goaded past caution. 'There's no difference whatsoever between my family and yours! Our house looks exactly the same as any other house in Renmark Street. And if you don't believe me, you may come along after school and see for yourself, you prying little zelph!'

'What's a zelph?' asked Dallas curiously, and X blushed, cross with herself for being needled into Zyrgonese gutter-talk.

'Can I really come to your house after school?' Michelle purred. 'Why, thank you, Charlotte.' She exchanged a gloating look with her friend Dallas.

'I didn't really mean . . .' X said, flustered.

'I don't have to ask my mother first. She doesn't get home from work till six. Oh, I can hardly wait to see your house!'

'Neither can I,' said Dallas. 'You did mean that I can come, too, didn't you? Michelle and I always go around together.'

X looked about helplessly, trapped by Community Centre training. It was considered very bad manners for an Organizer to debar anyone from entering an apartment if they wished to visit. Besides, she'd foolishly issued that invitation in the first place.

'Can I come, too, Charlotte?' a nicer voice asked. X looked at the speaker and received the comforting impression that Jenny Roland knew how nasty those two were, and was willing to act as a buffer to protect her from their wiles.

But she worried about the impending visit all through afternoon school. When the final bell rang, Michelle, Dallas and Jenny waited at the front entrance, and X just had time to whisper to Qwrk and Dovis, 'Emergency! We must all strictly follow the advice given about house guests.'

She led the way to the house, hoping desperately that everything would be in order there. Dovis wasn't at all concerned, her mind being fully occupied with her poem about summer kissing the hands of tired winter trees. X took the visitors around to the back door and into the kitchen, remembering that that was usual with school companions. Dovis went off somewhere to put her new poem to paper.

Everything in the kitchen looked innocuous and tidy. There was even a pleasant table decoration of flowers gathered from the garden. It looked no different from kitchen interiors in the PIC. Father wasn't there. He'd gone out, despite instructions.

'George, you'd better have your usual little after-school nap,' X said smoothly, wanting to get him out of the way. 'You know that Mother insists upon it.' Qwrk shot her a toxic look, but was wise enough to co-operate in an emergency situation.

'Yeth, Charlothe,' he said with a credible lisp. 'I'll go thalk to my theddy bear.'

'He's sort of cute,' Dallas said.

'Cute, but weird,' said Michelle. 'Today I heard he wrote down a list of way-out words no one ever heard of.'

Father had left a message on the kitchen table: 'X, gone to food shop. We don't have anything called Basil. Isn't that a person? It's one of the things I need for tonight's meal. Have gone to see if he or it is available at the store. Please tell Dovis not to fly with so much energy in main room. I dusted in there today.'

X hurriedly put the message into her pocket. On the table there was also a stack of coloured pictures of food, cut from magazines. They lay beside Qwrk's solar reckoner, which she also slipped into her pocket. 'Some little game of Qwrk's,' she said, as Michelle picked up a picture of oranges and another of poultry wrapped in foil. X guessed that Father had processed all those pictures through the reckoner to compose new and startling recipes of his own. The local food and its preparation had rather taken his fancy.

'I wish I had a little brother,' Dallas said.

'Yes, but a normal one,' said Michelle. 'My young sister's in George's class. She said he got up at Show and Tell and told the class how to repair a computer terminal if it breaks down.'

'With Father being an engineer, George must have picked up some of the terminology,' X said, and offered afternoon tea. Their eyes roamed about the kitchen like doodlestars, she thought resentfully. Only Jenny Roland didn't join in that blatant curiosity.

'It's been a pleasure,' said X when they finished the tea and biscuits. 'Don't let me detain you.'

'But we want to see over your house,' clamoured Michelle and Dallas. Jenny didn't say anything.

It was nerve-racking, showing them the rest of the house. When X opened the bathroom door, it was to find that Mother, apparently bored with the original white tiles, had altered them impulsively before she left to start her new job. The walls were now of transparent cubes, and in the centre of each cube cavorted a tiny living fish.

'Where did you buy those fantastic tiles?' cried Jenny. 'I never knew you could get tiles like that!'

'We know someone in the import business,' X said, shutting the door quickly. Mother, obviously, had taken recent, secret lessons in kinetics from Dovis. The bathroom tiles were from the modular on Zyrgon.

There was another bad moment in the hallway. X looked down at one of Aunt Hecla's hybrid-antelope fleecefur rugs. Mother must have been feeling extremely nostalgic before leaving for work. Hybrid fleecefur was thirty centimetres long, curled like springs, was whiter than the whitest imaginable snow, and retained its body warmth for several years. She waded grimly through the springy tendrils to the living room.

'Have you got central heating in this house?' Michelle asked, impressed in spite of herself. 'My feet feel warm. And the carpet. Where did . . .'

'We bought the carpet in Holland,' X said. 'They're quite common there. This is the main room.'

Dovis had written a poem on the ceiling in fluorescent pencil. X saw that it, too, was nostalgic, all about the glamour of Zyrgonese spaceshuttle pilots, but luckily it was in cryptic anagrammatic form.

'Funny wallpaper,' said Dallas, eying Mother's mural. She obviously thought that the spectrum curtains were funny looking, too, but Jenny Roland said they were lovely.

X noticed, filing her indignation away for later, various other objects that had been smuggled in. Mother had kinetized a trophy won by Father at Klickscore and placed it beside the television set. Father was proud of that trophy, because he'd been only seven when he won it, competing against wily herder types from the inner moon. It was a hideous trophy. X had never allowed him to display it in the apartment in Zyrgon. It was made of the same vulgar alloy used for zoomsleds and it was nearly as tall as Aunt Hecla. It struck all three sets of lunar hours with a metallic gong. Not only was it a time-keeper, but it could play strident chime-music to wake one at prescribed times. It also had a multi-calendar, a debts calculator, a list of all the Zyrgonese changes of government for the past three thousand ice-seasons, an instrument for removing flints from hybrid hooves, and a drinks dispenser for all-night games of Klickscore.

'We haven't seen your room yet,' Jenny said, quite nicely. 'I really like your home furnishings, Charlotte. They're so . . .'

'Weird,' said Michelle, staring at a hanging basket of plaid glassflowers Mother had hung on the back of the door. They tinkled softly when Michelle touched them, and prepared to chime the Zyrgonese Welcoming Anthem. X hastily opened the door and hurried the girls along to the room she shared with Dovis. Dovis was sitting on her bed writing and didn't hear them enter. X could tell that she was on the final draft of her summer poem.

She was pleased with the neat appearance of her part of the room. The bed was tidily made, and there was nothing on the side table except a small alarm clock, which she'd bought specially as the presence of one in a bedroom seemed almost compulsory. But it wasn't really needed in their household, as Dovis always rose at first light to celebrate the birth of each new day with song, dance, flight and poetry. X's wardrobe held her spare school uniform and two simple changes of clothing. She was accustomed to a frugal style of living. She glanced at Dovis's wardrobe and went cold with dismay.

The doors were wide open and it was crammed with Cosmic Flier audition clothes. X had no idea that Dovis had managed to materialize them in such a quantity. They crackled and sparkled with colour, so that the wardrobe itself seemed to pulsate. Fortunately, the girls had their backs turned, and she was able to usher them out of the room before they noticed Dovis's spectacular flame costume in particular.

'We mustn't disturb Dovis when she's doing her homework,' X said uncomfortably, closing the door. She thought of her own homework, and how difficult it was to fit in amongst her multiple chores.

'She certainly didn't do the right homework last night,' Dallas said. 'I know that Fiona girl in her class. For Geography they were supposed to learn a section about irrigation, but your sister got up and recited this peculiar poem about under-ocean travel instead.'

'We haven't seen your little brother's room yet,' said Michelle. 'What's all this gooey purple stuff around the door frame?'

X winced, having forgotten about Qwrk's invisible room sealer, which had apparently lost its potency. 'Fumigation,' she lied. 'George's room is being fumigated for wood borers. Now, although it has been a pleasure, I really must NOT detain you for one more minute.'

'Your house is kind of unusual,' Dallas said at the back door.

'Weird, you mean,' said Michelle.

'Goodbye, and thank you for the honour of your visit,' X said, and shoved them all outside, politely but firmly.

Straight into the arms of Aunt Hecla.

SEVEN

Aunt Hecla was eccentric-looking, even for Zyrgon's
second moon. She made all her clothes from raw fleecefur, and a faint scent of hybrids always hung about her
like a mist. She hadn't ever cut her hair in her lifetime,
using it as an extra cape for the chill winds that swept
about her ranch. She was taller than anyone, and had
arms as strong as girders.

'X! So this is where you all got to!' she cried in her
vast voice, resonant from bawling to flocks across wide
prairies. 'Such trouble I had finding you! That brute of a
Lox kept hedging and saying you were all in an air pocket
with the furniture. I had to bribe him before he'd utter. If
you'd wanted a good place to hide, you KNOW I would
have put you up in the stables, even though Carillon's
just had a litter of twelve. Great thundering zelphs, what
funny children!'

She stared curiously at Dallas, Michelle and Jenny, and
picked Michelle up for a closer look. Michelle dangled
speechlessly, and it was difficult for X to remain in command of such a situation. 'A relative,' she explained. 'My
aunt. These are some girls from the school we attend
now. Aunt Hecla, I think Michelle Hudson would like to
be put down. She has to go home. Her mother is expecting her.'

'Expecting her?' demanded Aunt Hecla. 'She looks well and truly born to me. But Lox said that things would be a bit strange here. Nice to meet you, young ladies, but go away now, SCAT, I want to talk to my niece.' She flapped her great hands, and the girls left, turning back to stare at her immense studded boots and cape hair. X pulled her inside and shut the door.

'I see your mother's trying to make this native hut homelike,' Aunt Hecla said, looking about with interest. 'I didn't know you were planning to bring along decorating stuff, or I'd have lent you a trailer. Oh my, is that one of their video screens? Any chance of seeing some tribal dancing?'

'Not right now,' X said ungraciously. 'Just how did you get here?'

'Ran up a little space-raft out of some lumber,' Aunt Hecla said. 'I found a good place to park it, too, nice grassed area just down the street. My, you have grown thin, X! Once all this is over, you're coming to stay with me and I'll fatten you up. Just to keep you going meanwhile, I brought along a flagon of Carillon's buttermilk.'

Unnecessary information, as X could smell it anyhow. She put the flagon in the laundry by an open window. Aunt had also brought along an antelope, fortunately housetrained and also drowsy, tucked into one of her enormous leather belt-pouches. Zeppy curled up on the hall rug, no doubt imagining that he was in the centre of a herd. He blinked long-lashed black eyes and went to sleep, making a soft, tinkling purr. Aunt Hecla yodelled for Dovis and Qwrk and hugged them as though she hadn't seen them in light years. Then she inspected the rest of the house and obviously didn't think much of it. Her ranch house was hewed out of rock, and so was the furniture.

'What's happening on Zyrgon?' X asked. 'Are the Law Enforcers still looking for Father?'

'Those zelphs,' said Aunt Hecla scornfully. 'They had the brashness to turn up at my place with a search warrant. That's how I knew something was going on. Upsetting poor little Carillon, and her trying to suckle twelve kids! I was so mad I sent them scurrying back to their raft with a few slugs from a meltgun in the seat of their uniforms. They said your father had to be taught a lesson, muddling the economy like that with all those lottery wins. It's not fair, I pointed out to them. Why him? EVERYONE has a little fiddle with the lottery system. "Not twenty-seven times in a row." they said. "Someone has to be made an example of." There's no money left in the government treasury, not after your father's big clean up. Just as well Lox got you out when he did, I suppose, though I wish it hadn't been so far away. X, would you have a spot of rockshine for your old aunty?'

'They don't drink it down here. I can offer you tea or coffee, though. Tea is very nice, but Mother says coffee is considered smarter. They drink coffee at the place where she has her new career. She's designing Wear.'

'Rather her than me. Not my idea of a career, I can tell you. Roundup was terrific this year, X, though I must admit I'm feeling my age. Busted a couple of ribs again, but carried on regardless. Just strapped them together with a strip of Permapress and got straight on with the job. I've three sets of long-horn twins this year, would you believe. The longest curled antlers you ever saw, triple spirals. They should fetch a good price at the yearling sales, though I haven't been able to breed any coloured fleeces. It's a big disappointment, that. People are getting sick and tired of white fleecefur. So, tell me, how are you getting along down here with the natives? Anyone suspect you yet?'

'No, but only because of my diligence,' X said. 'The others keep doing the most stupid, risky things. Such as smuggling possessions from Zyrgon without my permission. Clothes and such things.'

Dovis didn't react. She was too busy trying to tell Aunt Hecla about school, with such unusual enthusiasm that X stared at her in surprise.

'There's no use babbling on in poetry,' said Aunt Hecla. 'You know I can't stand the stuff.'

'All right,' said Dovis. 'School is pleasant. They have lovely verse forms on this planet, Aunt, and beautiful books. I wish we had such books on Zyrgon. I like school very much, although the clothes we have to wear are truly horrible! Apart from that, I think I can tolerate our exile very well.'

'Poetry,' grumbled Aunt Hecla. 'Unhealthy habit, and a waste of time. You should come to stay with me more, and get some good brisk exercise rounding up the antelopes. And how about the lad, then?'

'I don't like it as much as Dovis,' Qwrk said. 'Though there's a certain amount of challenge to be had from convincing people that I'm of a low mental age.'

'That reminds me,' X said severely. 'I've been meaning to have a word with you about that A list. I told you particularly that the objects must be simple ones.'

'But they were. I thought of the simplest ones I could. Autoxidation, for instance. We covered that in the very first week of Knowledge Bank.'

'Not everyone went to Knowledge Bank, you little snob.'

'They're still holding the professorship for him,' said

Aunt Hecla. 'Lox just told them Qwrk was engaged in important research into antelope mating-calls, but he'd be back to begin next semester for sure. They don't mind. Time means nothing to those academics at that high-faluting place. And you, X, how are you managing, my darling? I'm concerned about your peakiness. I should have brought along some milk curd, which is just the thing for enriching the blood.'

'Thank you very much, Aunt, but they have quite healthy food here. I'm all right. I'm managing. Why shouldn't I be?' X avoided her eyes, which were bright blue and set in a framework of weather wrinkles from gazing over raggedy horizons. She didn't want Aunt Hecla to guess the extent of her worries; it was a matter of pride. She rather hoped Aunt wouldn't be staying long. She brought with her too many reminders of their proper home. X found herself yearning suddenly for Zyrgon, where the only troubles were keeping one step ahead of the authorities, and making sure that Dovis didn't float about all night composing verse. She almost wished that she'd made Father undergo Detention, in spite of the public humiliation. At least things would have been familiar. And at least she wouldn't have to endure this separation from Lox.

Present cares droned inside her head. Where was Father now? He'd been gone a long time just to find out where you could get Basil. And there had been a peculiar document in the letterbox with a payment demand from someone called SEC. X had no idea what that meant, and would have to resort to the interminable checking of the PIC. And Miss Brewster was expecting the parents to consult her about special tuition for Qwrk: another problem that would have to be dealt with. And Dovis, quite likely to write a landscape sonata describing summer-ice glittering beneath the three moons of Zyrgon, and read it aloud to her class. Mother at the boutique, and though she'd promised not to speak eighteenth-century French to anyone there, she wasn't reliable. The worries buzzed around X's mind like the noisier crescendoes of H73Chok's loudest symphony.

'When this is all over, X, you must come and stay with me for a long holiday,' Aunt Hecla said, looking at her keenly. 'I'll save up some fun jobs for you. You can help me blast out that big rock-formation in the south pasture, and dredge out a new lake. We could do with another one.'

'I can't leave the family for any length of time,' X said. 'Even on Zyrgon. Besides, there'll be quite enough work for me to attend to when we get back. Mother will have a whole string of Fifth-Day Luncheons to celebrate, and I'll have to organize the guest lists and everything else. And I'll have to really work at keeping Father on a straight pathway. If Lox manages to get him pardoned, he's going to have to watch his step.'

'Hello, Hecla, old girl! This is a nice surprise!' said Father at the kitchen door. 'Sorry I'm late, X, a thousand apologies. I picked up your dear mother from the boutique after I did the shopping. Couldn't have her walking home on her first day at the job.'

Mother's eyes sparkled from her obviously successful day. She was wearing a new gown and had painted her face the way the local women did, with not one trace of gold. Aunt Hecla stared and gave one of her immense, braying laughs.

'How polite of you to drop in, Hecla,' Mother said rather coolly. 'Don't let us detain you. I'm sure you'll want to beam home in time for evening fodder.'

'Those lazy layabout casual workers I hired might as well earn their keep,' said Aunt Hecla. 'I'm in no hurry. I thought I'd stay and have supper here and catch up on all the gossip.'

'I'm sure the children will be delighted. I notice you've brought along one of your creatures, though X won't allow you to keep it in the hallway. You know how houseproud she is.'

'It'll have to stay there,' X said. 'The neighbours might see if I put it outside. And I don't think they have hybrid-antelopes down here.'

'You don't have to worry about his supper,' said Aunt Hecla. 'I brought along a nosebag. I'll just nip back to the space-raft and get it.'

'The raft!' X cried. 'I forgot all about that!'

'What's the matter?' Aunt Hecla demanded. 'I know it's not registered, but then, neither is yours, according to Lox. Anyhow, I'm a bit too long in the tooth to be slithering up and down transport beams, and besides, it's too chilly for that lurk this time of the season. Not a bad little raft, if I do say so myself. Only took a couple of hours to run up out of bits and pieces. I might take you for a spin later, if you've a fancy.'

'Where did you say you parked it?'

'Down the street in a little field. Oh, I guess you're worried someone might have noticed it! There wasn't anyone around when I landed, X, I made sure. I'm not in my dotage yet, girl!'

'Nevertheless, I'll go and check,' X said, and hurried down Renmark Street to the park. Aunt Hecla's raft was there, but no longer in one piece. It was in several smaller ones. There was a grassed slope in the park, and sliding down it on pieces of the raft were two rowdy little boys. Two more were using what looked like the rudder as a cricket bat.

'Do you know what that object was that you just dismantled?' X asked one of them.

'We're allowed,' he said. 'Just a pile of old junk someone left lying around. This here's OUR park, anyhow. Kids under ten only, says so on the noticeboard. So you beat it, sister!'

'I am not your sister,' X said thankfully, and went back to the house. Aunt Hecla took the news quite well.

'I'll just have to go back by transport beam, then,' she said. 'And put up with the rheumatism later.'

Father made a particularly delicious meal in honour of her visit. There were two different types of casseroles, an enormous salad studded with black olives, and some delectable things called Rum Babas. But Mother didn't linger at the table afterwards. She beckoned X urgently into the hall and said, 'Can't you please try to contact Lox now? Hecla unfortunately lowers the tone of any dwelling she's in. The sooner she's returned to Zyrgon, the better.'

'She's not doing any harm. It really was nice of her to come all this way to see us.'

'It's just the sort of wild, scatterbrained idea she'd come up with, you mean. Oh, I do wish she'd lower her voice!'

For Aunt Hecla was singing. Father had produced some bottles of a special celebration drink used on this planet, and it had made Aunt Hecla very jovial. She was singing all the Herder Guild songs she knew in a voice as powerful as a space hurricane. X inspected her through the glass door of the kitchen, rather concerned, now, about fitting her into a transport beam. She seemed to have expanded, like her voice. There even seemed to be more of her hair, swishing violently every time she threw back her head to laugh, spilling all over the table. Even her feet looked larger, if that were possible. Father was joining in all the choruses. He, too, appeared to like the local celebration drink.

'I see what you mean,' X said. 'I'd better contact Lox immediately.'

She went into the quiet of the main room. Her beam contact was superb, usually. The last time she'd contacted Lox, he'd come through as crisply as though he were standing in the same room.

'Hurry, X,' Mother urged. 'Your aunt's started to sing that dreadful ballad about the herder and his bonus shearing-cheque. I'd like her sent back before she gets to verse twenty-three.'

'I'm trying as hard as I can,' X said. 'Mother, I can't even raise Lox. For some reason, he's not answering. Get everyone in here to form a circle to boost the power.'

They came reluctantly, not being skilled at it, and apt to suffer minor electrical shocks within the circle. Aunt Hecla wasn't much help at all. She giggled through her masses of hair and insisted that Zeppy be a member of the circle. He wove ingratiating patterns amongst their feet, like a cat. X ignored him as best she could and concentrated on the beam, struggling through layers of static and interference. Dovis was nearly as much hindrance as Aunt Hecla. Her mind was still brimming with distracting rhyming couplets about blossoms.

'Lox?' X thought worriedly. 'Lox, where are you?'

And suddenly his voice came through, crackling and indistinct, but blessedly there. 'Oh, my beloved Lox!' X thought.

The thought beam seemed to have become tattered somewhere along its length. She tried to explain about Aunt Hecla, but Lox kept saying, 'What? Who's on the line?' He sounded incredibly vague and hazy, as though he wasn't concentrating.

'LOX!' yelled X. 'You can't be trying properly! You'll have to do much better than that if we're to get Aunt safely back to Zyrgon tonight! It's useless to expect HER to be of any assistance, either. She's at the moment . . . not herself.' She glanced at Aunt Hecla, who had finished all forty verses of the song about the herder's cheque, and had gone to sleep quite abruptly on the floor.

Lox's voice became more distinct. 'What's your aunt doing down there?' he asked, sounding not as concerned as he should be. X explained again about Aunt Hecla's raft being dismantled, but Lox scarcely listened.

'I've got news for you and yours, X,' he said, interrupting her feverish calculations for getting Aunt Hecla returned. 'No, I don't mean that your father's been pardoned. I haven't had time to work on that yet. I've become betrothed! To Jady, you know, that gorgeous girl who runs the Shuttle refreshment kiosk. Aren't you going to congratulate me?'

Congratulate him? X could hardly speak! A sudden heavy weight had settled upon her heart. She'd always avoided the possibility that Lox would one day get himself betrothed before she'd attained a proper age to propose to him herself.

'What's the matter with you, X?' he asked impatiently. 'You sound peculiar. Even your silence is vibratory.'

'Congratulations,' X said with appalling effort. 'Please convey my best wishes to that girl, if she's the one I think she is, that fat one who never gives the customers the right change because she's too busy flirting with all the male passengers, not to mention the Shuttle crew!'

Mother, thrilled about the news, pushed her aside and chattered enthusiastically down the beam for the best part of ten minutes, demanding to know what Lox was planning to wear for the ceremony. Then she realized that she wouldn't be there to attend, and wept copiously, enough to blank out the contact altogether.

'Good riddance!' X said testily. 'I'm not going to set up another beam, either. Aunt Hecla will just have to stay here overnight. Someone get a rug to put over her.' Zeppy was munching experimentally on a chair leg. She shoved him out into the backyard, not caring now if the neighbours saw him or not. Then she went to her room and got out her secret folder of Lox pictures, for she, too, had been guilty of contraband smuggling. She spread the pictures out and looked at them. He was so heartbreakingly handsome in his Shuttle uniform! True, most of the badges and medals decorating his tunic couldn't have been there officially – Lox had always been a bit devious, but she'd planned to reform him if he'd waited till she were old enough to propose. There was a wonderful picture of him piloting a flashy little rocket at a hobby rally, only he'd been disqualified before that race had even started. Father had been his manager then, and together they'd added a little extra something to the flight fuel.

It just wasn't fair that she'd been born in the wrong chronology and he thought of her as a child, and that he'd got himself betrothed to one of those frivolous Shuttle kiosk attendants. She was so depressed that she even thought of seeking Mother out to have a good cry on her shoulder, but that was out of the question.

She heard footsteps in the hallway and hurriedly

pushed the pictures back into the folder.

'X, dear, is there anything wrong?' Mother asked. 'You look very pale.'

I've had a headache all day, but it's nothing. I'm just tired, that's all.'

'You work so hard. We're very fortunate that he have an Organizer like you. I'll always look back with pleasure upon my happy, carefree years as a mother, with you in charge. And I'm sure your father feels the same. You are always so strong, capable and efficient.'

'I should tell you that the school has realized that Qwrk has an exceptional IQ,' X said, not feeling strong and efficient at all.

'Are they going to make him a professor down here, too?' Mother asked happily.

'They don't have five-year-old professors down here. They suggested that Qwrk go into a higher grade at school, but I don't think it's a good idea at all. It's too risky. He won't be content with being moved up one year, once it starts. He'll forget to be cautious and will show off the sum total of his knowledge. We'll have to think of an excuse to satisfy the school. Miss Brewster wants to discuss it with you and Father.

'Oh, but that's not necessary. You decide. I know we can leave the matter in your capable hands.'

X looked down at her hands. Capable was the kindest way to describe them, she thought. They weren't elegant, like Dovis's hands. Nothing about her appearance was elegant and she most certainly would never mature to look like that pretty girl at the Shuttle kiosk. It had been conceit on her part to be interested in someone as exalted as Lox.

Apathetically, she went to make her final evening

83

inspection of the house and its occupants.

'Why don't you watch this television programme with me, X?' Father said. 'It's very interesting. All about different methods of preparing food in something called aspic.'

'I have too much to do to watch television,' X said, and went to check Qwrk. He was listening to one of the new music tapes, which was surprising, for he never listened to music on Zyrgon.

'This planet's older music is interesting,' he said. 'This composer, for example, used perfect counterpointing, involving twelve different patterns. I've worked out how he did that. He took an instrument called a violin . . .'

'They teach that at Miss Brewster's school,' X said. 'It was in the prospectus. Listen, Qwrk, I've just had a convenient idea. What we must do is divert Miss Brewster's attention from your other abilities. You've never been interested in playing a musical instrument and you're sure to be abysmally stupid in that field, like the rest of us. If Miss Brewster sees that you're hopeless at some things, perhaps it will balance out the other. It's worth trying. I'll see her about violin lessons for you tomorrow . . .'

'I've no wish to learn a musical instrument!' Qwrk said indignantly. 'It's not my area at all. I'm listening to this tape now only from scientific curiosity. The humming of the stars in their mathematical beauty is quite good enough for me!'

'I am the Organizer!' X said. 'You'll do as I say! It won't hurt you to be in that music room for a little while each week. They won't scold you for being stupid, either. I heard Jenny Roland have a lesson today, and she was terrible, but the teacher didn't scold her. I expect that it's because students have to pay extra for music tuition, and

Miss Brewster must be glad of the money. Anyway, it's most important for you to show another side to the school authorities. A side of you that isn't intellectual at all.'

'It'll be so undignified!'

'We must all make psychological sacrifices.' X went outside to check that all was in order before preparing for bed. She looked up at distant bright stars, homesick for her own world, exasperating though it was. She certainly didn't belong here; none of them did. Exile was terrible, and it would be wonderful when the time came to return home.

No, it would not! Lox would have set up a cosy apartment for two, and etiquette demanded that she and her family call on him and that Jady at least once a week to play Klickscore! It would be dismal to return home!

Something stole up behind her and licked her ankle with a warm, dewy tongue. Zeppy. She felt so desolate that she picked him up for comfort. Zeppy chimed ecstatically, and she realized with annoyance that he was now firmly convinced that she was his mother.

EIGHT

'You know I haven't time to set up another transport beam before we go to school,' X said. 'And Zeppy can't be given the run of the house all day. He'll have to be confined to one room.'

'I won't have him in here nibbling my fireglow dancing dress,' Dovis said stubbornly. 'He's Aunt Hecla's responsibility, anyhow. Let her look after him.'

'I can't wake her up. She has something the PIC calls hangover. Qwrk . . .'

'Zeppy can't stay in my room, either. I've grown quite fond of that pink ruffled bed, and I don't want it chewed. Besides, you're asking for enough unselfishness from me, making me have violin lessons when I don't even want to.'

Zeppy took a fold of X's skirt between his little silver teeth and wouldn't let go.

'Smitten by your company,' Qwrk said. 'You'll just have to take him to school with you.'

'He'd look out of place, and Michelle Hudson would make more nasty comments. There's no choice but to keep him inside until I can arrange return transport with Lox.' X's voice stumbled over that name. She hauled Zeppy, still attached to her skirt by his teeth, into the kitchen. Father wasn't enthusiastic at the prospect of minding him. The table was cleared of the breakfast things, and he'd collected the ingredients necessary for his aspic dish. He looked as indignant as an astrologer bothered in the middle of drawing up an important horoscope. X prised Zeppy's teeth apart with the handle of a spoon and popped in a mandarin, then took the opportunity of slipping out of the house. She certainly didn't want him following her to school on his little clicking hooves, bleating in lovesick bell scales.

She almost looked forward to school, where the busy timetable would distract her from thoughts of Lox. It was a silly, childish infatuation, anyhow, and she must use all her self-discipline to put it out of her mind. Girls often fell in love with the uniform and glamour of the Space Shuttle pilots. At Community Centre there had even been a special group of girls who sent anonymous gifts of flowers, sweets and devotional letters. They'd hang about the depot and squeal if they caught a glimpse of any of the pilots. But X had always considered herself above such nonsense.

Dovis, too, had never joined a devotional group. In her case, it was the reverse; groups of boys and sometimes one or two Shuttle pilots, formed clubs of adoration and sent HER gifts.

At the school gates, X took Qwrk's hand in hers, although he objected strenuously. 'Co-operate and conform,' she said. 'Other girls bring their younger siblings to the prep grade in such a manner.

She walked him into his classroom and handed him over to the teacher. 'I told our parents about Miss Brewster's flattering offer of advanced tuition for George,' she said. 'They don't want him to have anything like that. They're quite content with your excellent teaching, Miss Delaney. However, they'd like him to learn a musical instrument. The violin. Could he start today, please?'

'I'm sure it could be arranged,' said Miss Delaney. 'Oh, what fun, Georgie! It's lovely to make pretty music. You'll be able to play "Happy Birthday" for anyone in this grade who is a birthday person.'

'My good woman . . .' Qwrk began wrathfully, and caught X's eye. 'Yeth,' he said. 'I can thcarthely wait.'

X went to her room and found another note on her desk. *Charlotte the Weirdest Jackson* was printed on the outside. At first she didn't intend to open it and pushed it aside. It lay there like a barb not meeting its target, but vexed by that insidious little white arrow, she unfolded the paper. It contained a derisive sketch of Aunt Hecla, large feet accentuated, hair flying, a bulge under her cape (luckily no one had guessed it was Zeppy) making Aunt Hecla look very fat. They'd written underneath: 'Eccentric old Jackson family custom – on meeting new people, lift them into the air and examine them under a strong light!'

The note was signed Michelle Hudson and Dallas Brookfield.

X's sense of obligation to safeguard every member of her family from mockery arose within her like a flame. Without even considering the matter, she focused her thought-power to Retribution. Michelle and Dallas immediately came out in large green spots that flickered like strobe lights.

They looked at each other and began shrieking. Everyone turned and began yelling, too. Miss Harrow did not. (She would make a very good manager of an all-night Klickstore Casino, X thought respectfully.) Miss Harrow just said calmly, 'You two girls had better come with me to the sick bay, although I'm sure those spots are only a mild heat rash. The rest of you stop making that ridiculous noise and get on with your work. I'm pleased to see that at least one girl in my form doesn't indulge in stupid hysterics. If Charlotte Jackson can continue quietly with her work, then the rest of you should be able to do so, too.'

She led Michelle and Dallas out. They were as white as bread in between the green spots, and X allowed herself a secret smile of triumph. She knew that the spots would fade in twenty minutes with no further effort needed on her part. Although spectacular, they were quite harmless and only psychologically painful. Interested discussion hummed around the classroom while Miss Harrow was absent.

'I bet they got that awful rash from guzzling chocolates,' someone said.

'Michelle thinks she's great because her father owns a chocolate factory.'

'She never shares any, either, only with Dallas.'

'It'll do them both good, to have acne for a while, even if it's green.'

X's triumph changed to alarm when she was summoned to Miss Brewster's office just after lunch. She thought that Miss Brewster must have somehow found out who was responsible for those spots, but when she entered the office, she found Qwrk leaning nonchalantly against Miss Brewster's desk. And Miss Brewster didn't look cross at all.

'I just wanted to see you about George's music lessons, Charlotte,' she said. 'His first lesson, which he had this morning, was quite extraordinary.'

X tried to get at Qwrk's thought to find out what had taken place, but he cunningly set up a molecular shield so she couldn't reach inside his mind at all. 'Good,' she thought with satisfaction. 'That air of nonchalance doesn't fool me! He must have been even more stupid than the worst student they have ever had. Miss Brewster is trying to find a tactful way to suggest that music for him would be a complete waste of time. And serves the little wretch right, being taken down a notch or two!'

'Charlotte, are you listening?' demanded Miss Brewster.

'I'm sorry if he was backward,' X said. 'He's never learned music before, but I'm sure if he tries hard he'll be able to play simple little melodies eventually. Something like that little song about ducks they sing in his class room.'

'Never studied music before?' Miss Brewster asked. 'That's what I called you in here to verify. Really, this is astounding! Our music teacher says that George was able to play a Mendelssohn violin concerto at his very first lesson!'

'I didn't even try very hard, either,' Qwrk said modestly. 'It just happened.'

'Charlotte, I must discuss this with your parents! George's education should be totally reconstructed. I'd like to make arrangements for someone from the Conservatorium of Music to hear him play. As he is apparently a prodigy . . .'

'I think there must be some mistake,' X said. 'George has ALWAYS been very stupid about music. This morning must have been a fluke and I'm sure that our parents wouldn't want any fuss made about the situation.'

'Being able to play Mendelssohn at one's first violin

lesson is certainly something to warrant a fuss,' Miss Brewster said tartly. 'Your parents must contact me as soon as possible. And George, don't play on the slide or anything dangerous during afternoon recess. We must take very good care of those hands of yours.'

Out in the corridor Qwrk said, 'I didn't even know I was a musical genius until I picked up that violin. There was a folder of music on a stand and I was just amusing myself while waiting for the teacher. Seeing if I could make some sense of all those little black dots. It's really easy, you know, like basic mathematics. I didn't realize the teacher was standing in the doorway listening, and there was no possible way I could retrieve the situation. I think I rather like the violin, primitive though it is. It makes a very nice sound, much more interesting than all that electrical gadgetry on Zyrgon. I'm quite looking forward to my next lesson. And in the meantime, they said I can borrow a violin from school to practise at home. Of course, I'll need one of my own, eventually.'

'You won't, because there won't be any more lessons! I'll tell Miss Brewster that Mother has changed her mind and doesn't want you to study music at all.'

'X, did you know that people spend huge sums of money for the best violins?' Qwrk asked, paying no attention. 'And that there are people who earn their living by standing up on a platform playing for an audience? They're the ones with natural aptitude. Like me, though I seem to have much more than natural aptitude. Genius, to be precise.'

'You can just take that conceited look off your face! It's a very good thing that we're going to be leaving soon. You'd become even more conceited than you are on Zyrgon if we stayed here!'

X marched back to her class, and found them on their way to the oval for something called Interhouse Aths Team Selection. She didn't know what that meant, but guessed it must be important, because everyone was so serious about it. Dallas and Michelle's short stay in the sick room hadn't dampened their self-esteem. X could see that they thought their skills better than anyone else's. They hurled an object called a discus and the instructor measured the length of the throw and expressed great approval. X couldn't see the point of hurling such a heavy thing into the air without purpose, so wasted no energy.

Miss Payne didn't express approval towards her at all. She was told crisply that to be included in a house team meant more effort. Miss Payne made a little mark against her name in the clipboard, and X could see that it was a negative one, a small black cross. She felt humiliated, and wished that she'd tried harder, even if the exercise had seemed pointless. It was degrading to earn a negative mark.

'Butterfingers,' Dallas jeered, too low for Miss Payne to hear. 'You certainly won't be chosen for any of the events, Charlotte Jackson. No one would be dumb enough to choose you.'

X considered green spots again, and perhaps even purple checks, but had no time to manufacture either. Miss Payne had set up a frame with a crossbar, and ordered people to leap over it one by one. The terrain of Zyrgon and its satellites was mostly even, with very few obstacles of any kind. X had rarely had a cause to jump over anything, so when it was her turn, she blundered and set the bar toppling. Miss Payne added another black cross against her name on the list. Dallas and Michelle tittered.

'Don't take any notice of them,' Jenny Roland whispered. 'I'm never chosen for the house sports, either.'

But Michelle and Dallas were so uncharitable that X yearned to have Miss Payne place a positive sign, a tick, beside her name for them to witness. It was a matter of honour.

So she was delighted to find that running ability was to be tested, because running was something she could do well, having learned it by herding on Aunt Hecla's ranch.

Michelle whispered insolently, 'I wouldn't even bother starting, Charlotte. You'll only make a fool of yourself again. Just sit down and have a nice rest.'

But when Miss Payne blew her whistle as a signal, X shot forward and stayed there, well in front of everyone else. She sped all the way to the finishing line and didn't look back once. There was no need. She knew that the others had covered only half her distance. It was gratifying to see Michelle's and Dallas's expressions, and also Miss Payne's. She wasn't even out of breath at the finish. Hybrid-antelopes became very skittish at pasture and could fly across the grass as fast as any bird through air. Herders just had to develop very good running ability.

Jenny showed her pleasure at X's success by grinning and jumping up and down. Her generosity was an admirable quality, X thought, touched. Aunt Hecla certainly had never praised her running skill; she'd just taken it for granted. Other girls also paid her compliments, and she felt suddenly confused, not used to being the centre of attention. In her household, Dovis with the beauty and Qwrk with his intellect had always captured that role.

'Very well, girls, you may go back inside and change,' said Miss Payne. 'I'll make my final decision for the teams later and notify the people concerned.'

'What exactly are Interhouse Aths?' X asked Jenny on the way back into school.

Michelle and Dallas sniggered. 'Fancy not knowing that! Talk about thick!'

'Talk about dense! She must have gone to school in the middle of a jungle!'

'Maybe her weird aunt held her up to the light so many times it's done something funny to her brain!'

'Tri-weekly green spots,' X decided, 'and perhaps the third lumbar vertebral grip as an overture!' But before she could switch to Retribution, Jenny deftly executed some movement of her foot so that Michelle and Dallas sat down very abruptly.

'Interhouse Aths,' Jenny said, walking on as though nothing had happened, 'is when the school houses – they're like teams and there are five of them – compete for the shield. You've been put into Green House, same one I'm in. You're bound to get chosen for the four-hundred metres, only you'll have to run against Michelle and Dallas. They're always in the house events. Charlotte, I've been meaning to ask you before, would you like to come to my place for afternoon tea? Your sister can take George home for once, can't she?'

X accepted, not knowing how to refuse such an invitation, and later, when they arrived at Jenny's house, she was plunged into bashfulness. It somehow seemed an intrusion, her going in there. Jenny's mother, however, didn't seem surprised at the appearance of a total stranger. She went on pouring tea from a brown pot and pulled another chair to the kitchen table. X sat down opposite Jenny's three brothers. Mrs Roland asked kindly questions about school, and X discovered that Jenny had told her she'd lived overseas. She felt rather sorry that the deception must be sustained, for Mrs Roland's face was as sweetly innocent as a young child's. It seemed wrong to lie to her when she so obviously believed everything she was told. And Jenny's older brother, Colin, seemed to be staring across the table quite a lot. Perhaps he could guess she was lying, X thought worriedly. There was certainly nothing guileless about his face.

Flustered by his inspection, she looked away. The kitchen was very untidy and she wondered how Mrs Roland could sit there so placidly, not noticing. There was a large pile of unwashed dishes, spider webs on the ceiling, sandals lying by the door, and not one neat head of hair in the room. Her fingers ached for a comb. Even Mrs Roland's hair was just caught back with a rubber band. No member of the family rose to restore order. They just lounged about the table talking noisily.

'You're a very quiet girl, Charlotte,' Mrs Roland said. 'I envy your mother. My lot never stop talking, as no doubt you've noticed.'

'I speak only when necessary,' X said awkwardly.

'Her sister Astrella knows a lot of poetry off by heart,' Jenny said. 'And her little brother is a musical genius. They found out today and everyone at school was talking about it. Charlotte has an aunt who's taller than anyone, with hair nearly down to her ankles.'

X tried to change the subject. 'I see that the plaster's cracked in those walls,' she said. 'Perhaps your house foundations have shifted during the dry season.'

'You should see the walls at Charlotte's house!' Jenny said. 'They're lovely, all different colours. Her whole house is really interesting inside.'

'The traffic is heavy along this road. They should have a

central monitoring system, instead of allowing people to drive anywhere and at any speed,' X said.

Colin was definitely staring at her, she decided uncomfortably, and was glad when Jenny suggested that they go to her room. It was the first alien bedroom X had been in, though it didn't look much like the bedrooms in Renmark Street, furnished so carefully from the available data. None of Jenny's furniture matched the next piece. Instead of a desk, she had an old table, its surface badly scratched and stained. Every centimetre of it was covered with unrelated objects, stamps, shells, stuffed cloth animals, pencils in a jar, a ceramic pig with a hole in its back. X longed to tidy up, but knew it would be considered bad manners to touch another person's belongings.

'What do you usually do after school each day?' she asked curiously.

'The usual. Come home, have afternoon tea, listen to the radio. If I can be bothered I do my homework before dinner, otherwise I let it go till later.'

'And what do you do after dinner?'

'Same as everyone else, of course. Watch TV if there's anything good on, finish off my homework, stuff like that.'

X found herself envying Jenny's carefree lifestyle. Nothing was expected of her, she carried no burdens. Girls on this planet had a singularly relaxed time. X sighed, thinking of all the duties that awaited her at home. 'I must go now,' she said.

'Oh, must you, so soon? I was going to play my new album for you.'

'I'm sorry. My aunt's leaving tonight and I have to be there to say goodbye. And I think I must say goodbye to your mother. It's usual, isn't it?'

96

Mrs Roland, too, seemed genuinely sorry that she had to leave so soon. And Colin. He looked . . . disappointed. It was all very odd, X thought, puzzled. People on Zyrgon scarcely ever commented upon the goings and comings of Organizers.

'Pop in again, Charlotte,' Mrs Roland said. 'I'd like to hear more about your life overseas. Mind that you go straight home, now, so that your mother won't be worried.'

There was no way to explain, X thought, that in her household, Mother NEVER worried about her. It was the other way around.

NINE

Mother's curtains now had scalloped edges, each scallop the exact half-moon shape of Zeppy's teeth. The floors were studded with fruit cores and little cloven hoof-prints, and the walls with antler marks. Zeppy, in a tipsy trance of welcome, pealed enchantment at X's return.

'I think you could have kept an eye on him, Aunt Hecla,' she said grittily. 'Just look at all the mischief he's done!'

'No need to make such a fuss,' Aunt Hecla said. 'That school must be a right miserable old place to send you home so sour. You shouldn't scowl so much, and you haven't even admired my new hairstyle yet, either.'

'That's enough to make anyone scowl! What are they going to think when you turn up at the ranch like that? Everyone living on Zyrgon's second moon keeps their hair long because of the weather. I thought you'd stay in the house all day, judging by your condition when I left this morning. Now I see that it's just not feasible for me to take even a few minutes off duty!'

'Your father found this marvellous recipe called Prairie Oyster Pick-Me-Up. Terrific stuff! It really got me going again. Let me make you a Prairie Oyster, X. You look as though you need one, if that long face is anything to go by.'

'I'm all right,' X said. She tried to ignore the peculiar headache that had been stalking about her forehead during the day. It apparently couldn't be vanquished by willpower alone, and was becoming increasingly difficult to put up with.

'After I had a couple of Prairie Oysters, your father took me out to see the sights,' Aunt Hecla said. 'I put a coat on over my shearing clothes, so you needn't fuss. And I know the haircut was impulsive, but I never could resist a bargain-price offer. They had a notice up: *style/cut, half-price today only.* And what's more, X, they were so struck with my long hair they bought it to make up into a wig. I felt a bit like one of my own antelopes, being able to sell fleece like that. And don't worry about repercussions. When I get back, I'll just tell everyone I caught my hair accidentally in a pair of shearing clippers. Anyhow, I really do like it short. Such a novelty! Such a sense of freedom!'

'I think your hair looks lovely, all short and feathery and tinted blue,' Dovis said. 'While you're here, you could also get your fingernails painted red.'

'Whatever for, child?'

'People just do, and you can buy other beautiful fingernail colours, not just gold, as on Zyrgon. I'll just have to take a supply back with me.'

'Are you mad, Dovis?' X said. 'As if we could explain red fingernails when we land!'

'People on Zyrgon are too fond of sticking their noses into other people's affairs,' Aunt Hecla said suddenly. 'That's why I retired to the second moon, only that's chock-a-block full of nosey parkers, too, now. It's a shame, really. X, you should relax a bit more and let everyone enjoy themselves while you're all down here in exile. There are certainly some interesting things. We

99

had a splendid drive around town in that vehicle! I wouldn't mind taking one back to the ranch with me.'

'Completely out of the question! And speaking about returning, I'll beam Lox now to set up a transport.'

'Oh, but I don't want to go just yet,' Aunt Hecla said. 'I want to stay and taste some of that aspic stuff your father's been preparing. There's plenty of time, X. After supper will do.'

'If I wait till after supper, I might not have enough strength to set up a beam,' X thought, suddenly anxious. The headache wasn't confining itself to her forehead. She became aware that her legs felt tired and heavy, and had been so all day, even though she'd run so successfully at school. The best Organizers never allowed themselves to be ill. Perhaps it would just go away if she disregarded it.

But you couldn't disregard a sneeze. Not one as gigantic as that.

'X!' Aunt Hecla said reproachfully. 'Is that one of their gutterwords? If so, you've no call to use it on your old aunty.'

'I didn't say anything. That was something called a sneeze, and I think I might be developing one of the indigenous ailments. The local treatment for viral illness consists of bed-rest with plenty of fluids to drink. Just to be on the safe side, Aunt Hecla, I'll beam you back now, while I'm still able.'

'Nothing doing,' said Aunt Hecla. 'I certainly won't leave if you're coming down with some nasty foreign disease. I'll stay here and help you attend to your household.'

'I can manage perfectly well on my own, alien virus or not! I certainly shan't give in to illness! I'll go to school as usual and continue to supervise this family.'

'You can go ahead and set up a beam if you want,' Aunt Hecla said stubbornly. 'I certainly won't get into it, and Zeppy won't, either, if I tell him not to. I'm staying until you look a whole lot better than you do now, and that's final. Anyhow, X, all this zeal about setting up beams; it wouldn't have anything to do with a certain pilot, would it? I'd forget about him, if I were you. Much as you might like to hear the sound of his voice, he's well and truly betrothed to that dizzy girlfriend of his. No loss to you, child, either. That Lox would make a terrible husband, always spending his salary on fancy new uniforms and preening in front of mirrors. And no scruples worth mentioning. A different girlfriend on every planet and satellite in the galaxy, I shouldn't wonder. I've always been thankful he's that much older than you so some other poor idiot would nail him down and make him go through a ceremony before you got any bright ideas.'

X felt her cheeks flame with embarrassment. She went haughtily into her own room and shut the door. It was appalling that anyone had guessed that infatuation! She sat miserably on her bed, fighting for composure, and listened to the sounds of the household: Father setting the table for the evening meal; Mother coming home from the boutique; Dovis dancing blithely in the hallway; Aunt Hecla trying unsuccessfully to coax Zeppy out of the refrigerator. She knew that she ought to be out amongst them to supervise the early evening routine, but she didn't have the energy to supervise anything. She was feeling distinctly worse by the minute, and the bed looked a haven of comfort.

She found herself taking off her school clothes and getting into pyjamas. She folded back the bedspread and slipped in between the smooth sheets. 'Just for a little space of time,' she thought hazily.'No more decisions. They can manage for themselves, for half an hour, anyhow. They'll just have to get along without me.'

But it was much longer than half an hour. When she awoke, Father was standing by the bed with a tray of food. 'It's morning,' he said. 'We didn't disturb you, because you looked so ill. Mother's gone to work and the others to school. Here's some breakfast, poor X.'

X was so horrified at not waking in time to get everyone's day organized that she could hardly eat, although Father had prepared the tray beautifully, even to a little golden flower tucked into a glass.

'The PIC says you should remain in bed till your temperature stabilizes, whatever that means,' he said. 'Qwrk calculated that you have an ailment called influenza, but don't be distressed. We'll look after you.'

'But I'm supposed to be looking after all of you! I can't possibly stay in bed!'

'Influenza can sometimes turn into something terrible called pneumonia,' said Father. 'Besides, I telephoned the school and told them you'd be away for a few days. You see, I can be efficient when it's necessary. Miss Brewster was perfectly charming. She says there's a lot of this transferable influenza about, and not to worry about missing school work.'

'And the violin lessons?' X asked anxiously. 'Did you do as I told you and cancel them?'

'All that has been taken care of.'

Father took the tray away and X tried to sleep, but it wasn't a healing sleep. She kept half-waking, restless and unhappy at being in bed during normal waking hours. Zeppy had found his way into the room and was curled up, tinkling gently, at the foot of the bed. He'd gobbled the decorative fringe from the spread.

'You just wait till I get enough energy for a beam,' X thought irritably. 'You'll be zapped back to your satellite so fast it will make your ringlets uncurl, you little pest!'

Lox, she thought aggrieved, could have easily set up a beam from his end, now that he realized she'd been landed with Aunt Hecla and Zeppy. It surely wasn't asking too much. People always seemed to leave everything to her. She started to think of his betrothal ceremony, with that odious Jady smirking and clinging to the arm of his best silver uniform. It would be painful having to visit them on Fifth Days and she didn't know how she was going to bear it!

During the long idle hours she listened for reassuring sounds that would mean that things were still running smoothly. It was easy to keep track of Aunt Hecla. She and Father seemed to have plenty of gossip to catch up on, and X wished rather crossly that they would do so in the same room. But in the afternoon Father announced that he was going shopping and would take Aunt Hecla with him, and the house grew blessedly quiet. X relaxed a little and became aware of how comforting bed was. It was very pleasant to lie there and not have to bother about Qwrk and Dovis for the present. Soon enough, she thought, they would come home from school, fretting and tense from a whole day of having to manage without her. They were so dependent. They'd dissolve into tears, probably, as soon as they set foot in the house, and she'd have to find the strength to solve any problems that might have arisen.

But their homecoming wasn't like that at all. Qwrk just went straight to his room and she heard the sound of a violin playing. 'Such disobedience!' she thought furiously. 'He should have returned that violin to the school, now that he no longer has lessons. I suppose he thinks Miss Brewster will just forget about it!'

Dovis didn't come inside straight away, but stayed at the front gate, talking to a couple of girls from her class. X struggled out of bed, alarmed at how weak she felt, and went to the window to listen. She could hear pieces of the conversation. 'And Louise said to Wendy...and then Gabie turned around and said that Lou hadn't meant that at all, what she meant was...I heard from Barbara that...'

X went back to bed, relieved. That was just the way everyone in Dovis's class conversed with one another, and it was fortunate that Dovis had learned the technique so quickly. She hadn't rhymed any of the words, and she'd even uttered an occasional loud, screaming giggle, just like those other girls.

After a while she came inside. 'Greetings, X,' she said cheerfully. 'Lynne has lent me three of her music tapes, though they aren't called that, did you know? The PIC's wrong on that point, they're called cassettes. I'll take the stereo, not called the music-machine by the way, into the main room. I don't want to disturb you when you're so ill. Oh, I suppose I should ask if you're feeling any better?'

But she'd gone without waiting to be told. X lay back on the pillows, feeling strangely annoyed. She almost wished that Dovis and Qwrk HAD come running to her with tears and problems. It was eerie, being left alone and apparently not even needed. And when Father returned, he didn't come to her room to report, either. He and Aunt Hecla were making themselves coffee in the kitchen. Zeppy awoke, pricked his ears and scrambled down from the bed chiming for pears, and like an echo, the front door bell rang.

'Miss Brewster, probably, come to reclaim that violin,' X thought. 'Maybe accompanied by one of their Law Enforcers.'

But Jenny Roland appeared at the bedroom door. 'Astrella told me at school that you had the flu,' she said. 'So I thought I'd drop in and visit. Your father said it was okay to come straight in. Here, I brought you this.'

X removed the paper wrapping and found a small bright sphere with facets of numbered colours. 'What is it for?' she asked, bewildered. All the gifts she'd ever received in her life had been useful, practical things. This particular one seemed to have no purpose whatever.

'Why, Charlotte, don't you know? It's a colour puzzle. You mix it up and then try to get the numbers back in the right order.'

X saw immediately just how to solve it, but instinct told her that it would be somehow ungracious to show Jenny that she knew. She pretended to watch while Jenny slid the little tabs about, but even though its structure was so simple, her delight in receiving it wasn't spoiled. It was the first useless thing she'd ever owned in her life.

Jenny suddenly picked up something lying on the end of the bed. It was a picture of Lox, which had slipped from the secret folder. 'Who's this?' she asked. 'It's a peculiar uniform. Is he a hotel doorman or a stunt motor-cyclist or something?'

Fortunately there wasn't anything incriminating in the background, apart from the hull of a Space Shuttle Inter-galactic Starship, which merely resembled a metal wall. Lox was posed against it, looking, X thought wistfully, quite splendid and dashing.

'He's got a nice smile,' Jenny said. 'A bit old, though.'

'He's only twenty-nine,' X said indignantly, quickly converting to solar years.

'Oh, a friend of your father's then, is he?' Jenny said, losing interest. She sat cross-legged on the bed, making herself at home in a way that would have been quite unthinkable on Zyrgon. 'Charlotte, you've just got to get over the flu by next Tuesday,' she said, 'because you're running for Green House in the Interhouse Aths! Miss Payne put up the list this morning and you're in the four-hundred metres. Dallas and Michelle are, too, and you should have heard the way they carried on when they saw your name! But everyone in Green House will be barracking for you like crazy . My mum will; she always manages to come to the sports. Maybe your parents will be able to take time off from work, too. Miss Payne was very impressed about how fast you could run and your style and everything. I heard her talking to one of the other teachers in the corridor.'

'Did she?'

'Of course. Why do you act so surprised about it?'

'I'm not used to people praising me, that's all.'

Father came in with a plate of beautifully decorated small cakes. 'It's not every day we're honoured with such a charming visitor,' he said. 'I ran up a few petit-fours, but I hope I didn't use too much crème de menthe in the green ones. You must tell me of any faults, for I trust your judgement implicitly.'

'In a minute he'll be kissing her hand,' X thought.

'Father, I can smell something burning in the kitchen,' she said crisply and effectively.

'It must be great having a dad interested in cooking. These cakes are terrific! He should be a chef instead of an engineer, if he can cook like this . . .' Zeppy shot into the

106

room and landed in Jenny's lap with a flying leap. 'Oh, where did you get this, whatever it is?' she cried. 'From overseas? It looks like a unicorn!'

'It's just a hybrid, a type of miniature crossbreed goat,' X said hastily. 'It belongs to my aunt, but it won't be here long. Not after tonight. My aunt's leaving tonight and the goat will be going with her.'

'But Charlotte, you said your aunt was leaving last night! That's why you had to rush home in a hurry before I even had the chance to play my new album for you . . .'

'There were last minute transport difficulties. But tonight she's definitely leaving,' said X. 'As you had better,' she thought, troubled. 'If Aunt Hecla strolls in and sees how much you admire that wretched little Zeppy, she's quite likely to present him as a gift. With a whole lot of rash anecdotes about life on a moon ranch.'

'Thank you for your visit, Jenny,' she said. 'If you've finished the cakes, I think perhaps it's time you went.'

Jenny's face changed. She got off the bed and went to the door.

'I've hurt her feelings,' X thought. 'I wish I'd chosen other words.'

'I hope you don't think I was being pushy or anything, coming to see you,' Jenny said. 'I wouldn't have come, if I'd known you didn't want me to. I just thought you might be feeling a bit lonely, stuck in bed with flu and not knowing anyone. It's horrid, being new at school. Being new anywhere. But I expect it's different for you. You obviously don't want to be friends with anyone!'

'Why did that nice young lady leave so soon?' Father asked, coming in with coffee served elegantly on a silver tray. 'I was going to invite her to stay for dinner. You know, that's rather a delightful local custom, being able to ask people informally for meals, instead of all that ridiculous Zyrgonese fuss about Fifth-Day Luncheons and those complicated guest lists . . .'

'I think it's a silly custom and I'm glad it's confined to this planet,' X said stonily. 'Those girls at school are forever in and out of each other's houses, as far as I can see. It's called being best friends. And it has nothing whatever to do with me.'

TEN

She was still too ill to go to school the next day.

'Better get you some hybrid milkcurd,' Aunt Hecla said. 'Dovis, kinetize Carillon and her litter down here right now. We can easily turn that vehicle into a make-shift stable.'

'No more objects, animals or people from Zyrgon,' X said. 'This illness will run a natural course and go away all by itself if I stay quietly in bed. Without anyone causing me any worry.'

'Oh, we won't!' everyone said virtuously.

'Return that violin today, Qwrk,' X added. 'You should have done so yesterday. It's pointless keeping it, now that Father's cancelled the lessons.'

'I will,' Qwrk said, but didn't. When he came home from school, X could hear him playing it in his room again. And Father seemed to spend an inordinate amount of time out of the house, taking Aunt Hecla with him, but she felt too jaded to investigate. She promised herself that she'd sort everything out when her strength returned.

But that didn't happen until the evening of her fifth day in bed. Feeling much better, she sat up and prepared to exert her authority. 'Just what have you been up to, Father?' she demanded. 'It can't have taken so much daily time to do the shopping.'

'I've been showing Aunt Hecla around,' Father said evasively. 'She found a place where they play a game called Bingo and she won a lot of money. No, she didn't use Qwrk's reckoner. I told her you wouldn't approve. And apart from Bingo, we've just been sightseeing. It's quite all right. Mother bought some clothes from the boutique so Aunt Hecla would look just like everyone else. She's out at that hall where they play Bingo right now, and won't be home for dinner. X, don't nag her about going back just yet. Poor old Hecla hasn't had a decent break from the ranch for a long time. She's enjoying this stay with us, and besides, it would be cruel to send her back until she sees you fit and capable and on your feet again.'

'Which, I'm thankful to say, seems to be happening now. I think I'll get up for dinner.'

'Oh, but we're managing splendidly! You mustn't rush things. There's another matter, X, which I should mention. I think I'll get myself a proper job while we're in exile. Everyone else in this street seems to have one.'

'We discussed all that, Father. Mother earns enough to support us, and we shan't be here much longer, anyhow. It's best that you stay in the house.'

'Mr Reagan in the next house is a Plumber,' Father said wistfully. 'He has a special vehicle with his name on the side. And Mr Deane at number six is a Company Manager. That's a very impressive title. He has something called an Expense Account. I want to be a Manager with an Expense Account. I won't ever get the chance when we're back on Zyrgon; Mother wouldn't let me. But she says she doesn't mind if I get a job while we're living down here. She's changed her mind about that, as it's the local custom.'

'It has nothing to do with Mother! You take your orders from me, as I shouldn't have to remind you! Oh, I knew I shouldn't have stayed in bed, in spite of my illness. There's a certain air of dissidence in this house . . . you and Mother chatting about jobs behind my back . . . Aunt Hecla pretending to be a native . . . Dovis coming home late . . . Qwrk with that violin . . . why haven't you made him give that back to Miss Brewster?'

'He needs it,' Father said. 'Besides, it's not the one belonging to the school. I went out and bought him one of his own. That school instrument was very inferior, according to the gentleman from the Conservatorium of Music who is giving Qwrk lessons now. How proud I am to have a musical prodigy for a son! That's what his new teacher says he is. And that's another reason why I should get a job. Those violin lessons are very expensive, even with the money your aunt donated from her Bingo winnings.'

Dovis came in, did something to her hair in front of the mirror, and headed blithely for the door.

'Where are you going?' X asked.

'To a delightful place called a pizza parlour. Lynne and I are meeting two charming people there, David Carruthers and Trevor Smeeton. David has brown eyes and remarkable eyelashes and a skin tanned gold by the sun. I could write a sonnet about him, but I don't have much time for poetry lately. He's been walking home from school with me since you've been confined to this room. I must say that I prefer his company to yours, X, though I don't mean to be tactless.'

'You are NOT going to anything called a pizza parlour to meet people I haven't yet investigated!' X said. 'Telephone that Lynne girl and make some excuse . . . And

Mother, if that's you out there in the hall, why are you so late? You're expected to arrive home punctually at five forty-five.'

'Well, I couldn't today. The owner of the boutique, Andrea Purnell, offered me a half-ownership and we were discussing the final details. I can easily get something called a bank loan to finance my share. Your father explained it all to me. He's developed a very good head for figures since we've been living down here. Oh, just think! Me, actually owning a boutique halfway across the galaxy and turn left!'

X pushed aside the bedclothes and stood up, relieved to find that the room no longer spun. She showered and dressed, put on her sternest expression, and went to inspect the household to find out just what had taken place during her absence. Zeppy's trail could be followed as easily as though tracking him through snow. There were chunks bitten out of almost everything; he'd even nibbled small archways at the base of each door so he could leave and enter every room at will. The lower halves of all the bedspreads resembled lace and the floors were littered with chinaware bitten into mosaics. Zeppy had apparently liked the blue and white and patterned china best. X tracked him to a cosy nest he'd made by burrowing deeply into the couch upholstery. The burrow was lined with the shredded remains of her school blazer. Zeppy blinked and yawned when she scolded him, and it was obvious that he was preparing to go into hibernation.

Dovis, sprinkled lavishly with Mother's French perfume, was on the point of leaving the house by stealth and the back door. X yanked her back inside. 'Your presence is required at a family council!' she said, and pushed

Dovis into the kitchen. She had difficulty getting Qwrk there, as he refused to be parted from his violin, but she managed to dump both into a chair at the table.

'Must we have a boring old council right at this minute?' Mother asked without enthusiasm. 'I've got some marvellous ideas for leisure suits. Andrea and I thought we'd make them as a new autumn theme, to celebrate our partnership. If I can just jot some designs down on paper . . .'

'Sit!' X ordered, and Mother did so, very unwillingly.

X noticed that Father had bought himself a ridiculous tall white cap and an apron, which she told him to remove at once. He obeyed, but looked for a minute or two as though he were planning otherwise.

Dovis was muttering to herself. X listened and deciphered a string of rhyming couplets, all very unflattering and all about herself. Qwrk set them to violin music, grinning.

'Silence!' X said. 'This council will now begin.'

'I'm not used to being ordered about at the boutique,' Mother said resentfully. 'Even Andrea defers to me there. She's very impressed that I can speak French and she can't. I daresay that I could end up as full owner of that boutique one day, with HER working for ME. That is, if I'm not hounded constantly by autocracy in my off-duty hours.'

'I just hope this silly meeting doesn't go on too long,' Dovis said. 'I really do have to see David. He's asked me to something called a cricket match on Saturday afternoon, and we have to make final arrangements. And there's no need to look so disapproving, either, X. That's what girls of my age do down here; they go to various places with boys like David Carruthers. You've done nothing but advise me to conform, ever since we landed, and I am conforming, so there!'

'I'll have something to say about David Carruthers later, but the first item on my agenda is the matter of Qwrk being allowed violin lessons with a private teacher. Without my permission!'

'You mustn't take very long over this council,' Qwrk said. 'It's vital that my practice-hours aren't interrupted. Mr Hohenhaus, my new music teacher, said so. He's drawn up a very strict schedule, which I want to adhere to, because I'd like to be the best violin player on this planet. And it's not conceit, either. I really like that instrument and its music, and I'd much rather be excellent than mediocre. Mr Hohenhaus says that I already have the talent, but something else called technique must be mastered. I don't mind how hard I have to work. It's much more interesting than anything I ever studied on Zyrgon. Mr Hohenhaus . . .'

'Qwrk, I don't want to hear any more! You've all been babbling emotionally over various matters, when it should be perfectly obvious that we mustn't form attachments to things and people down here. You were supposed to keep yourselves detached. Like me. Just what is going to happen if you come out with remarks about violins and boutiques when we're back on Zyrgon? Or if Dovis happens to mention David Carruthers . . .'

'I don't like being called Dovis anymore. My name's Astrella.'

'Not for very much longer! I've come to a decision. I'll beam Lox tonight and ask him to bribe one of the officials so we can go back immediately. We won't wait for a change of government. There's my money in storage that I had from winning the Community Centre Organizing

Scholarship. It should be a large enough bribe to get us a landing site and an official pardon within twenty-four hours. Now, isn't that good news?'

There was a sudden odd silence around the table.

'Mother?' X said, puzzled. 'Didn't you hear what I just said? In twenty-four hours you'll be on the way home. Just think, soon you'll have your moonchip tumblers out of the air pocket and be having a lovely time fielding all Mrs Gombaldu's curious questions about where you've been lately.'

'Andrea and I will be doing the window display the day after tomorrow,' Mother said stiffly. 'It won't be convenient to go back beforehand.'

'And I'll be at the cricket match with David Carruthers,' said Dovis. 'It's not convenient for me, either.'

'It's never going to be convenient for me,' Qwrk said. 'Not now. I've got to stay here until I finish my music studies. No one on Zyrgon knows anything about violins.'

'I thought you'd all be overwhelmed with delight about going home!' X cried wrathfully. 'You made enough fuss about having to come to here for exile! I don't like this at all, and the longer I allow you to remain here, the worse these infatuations are going to get. It's my duty as an Organizer to make sure that you remain loyal to Zyrgon and its government. At least to whichever government happens to have bribed itself into power for a couple of weeks. I learned that in my course at Community Centre.'

'You didn't learn it,' Qwrk said. 'You were just told of it. There's a difference. No one ever learns anything properly on Zyrgon. They should have Mr Hohenhaus there, if they want to know what proper teaching is all about.'

'X, I'm afraid I can't see my way clear to going back tomorrow evening, either,' Father said apologetically. 'I'm sorry, but it's just not possible. I was going to tell you when I found enough courage, but I suppose you'd better know now. Everyone else does. Tomorrow evening is the opening of my new restaurant. I bought it with the money I won at the gambling races, which you put in that air pocket, but Aunt Hecla zapped it all back again while you were in bed. She was a little rusty, but remembered how to do it. You must admit, X, that the money was going to waste there. I'm going to be chef as well as the manager at my restaurant, and you can scold as much as you like, but I won't listen. You can send me to my room in disgrace, but I don't care about that, either. I'll just get on with planning my menu. This is the only chance I'll ever have to be a proper chef and I'm going to make the most of it. I don't want to go back to Zyrgon sooner than we have to. Oh, just wait until you see my little restaurant! Hecla's been helping me get things ready. The Hybrid-Antelope, it's called, and we're using Zeppy for interior decoration. He won't mind, now he's in hibernation. Hecla often just stores her hybrids on shelves to keep them from getting underfoot when they're like that. Mind you, I have no bookings yet for the opening night, only the family, but it won't take long to build up a clientele. Not with my cooking skills.'

'Oh, X, don't look at him so sternly,' coaxed Mother. 'Why can't we all have a bit of fun while we're here? And you shouldn't waste money on a bribe to get us home, either. Just wait for a change of government, as Lox suggested. We'll be back on Zyrgon soon enough, anyhow, dreary old place that it is,' she added to herself.

X stared around the circle of faces, shocked into

silence. In the silence, Mother picked up her sketch pad and began to jot down ideas for designs, as though nothing else mattered; Qwrk went off to his room with his violin; Father put the white cap jauntily on his head; and Dovis defiantly kinetized herself away to the pizza parlour.

X left the table and went into the living room, where she emptied her mind of everything except concentration. The beam sliced immaculately through the atmosphere, across the vast cold oceans of space and into Lox's apartment on Zyrgon. It was a superb, beautiful beam, sparkling with clarity.

'I wish you wouldn't do that without preliminary warning, X!' Lox said crossly. 'You made me spill medal polish on my uniform!'

'Forget about sartorial splendour, and listen carefully,' X said.

Lox listened.

'I think you're over-reacting,' he said when she'd finished. 'There's no need to throw your weight around and order them back, poor things. You might consider me a little, too. It's going to be a bore, arranging a bribe, just when I'm in the middle of having fittings for my betrothal uniform. Gold, it's going to be, with marvellous epaulets in multi-colour. Jady designed it. We're having the ceremony in the Shuttle kiosk. Noisy, but impressive . . .'

'I don't want to hear all about that! You must go straight out and arrange the bribe. Try to get the central landing-bay, as that raft is so clumsy to manoeuvre, especially if I'm going to have a whole lot of mutinous people on board to contend with. We shall be leaving tomorrow nightfall, Lox, and you must have everything in order at your end.'

'It's very inconvenient, but I suppose I shall just have to do it, if you're in such a state. X, it goes without saying that no one must suspect where you've been. Remember that you've all been hiding in a cave or an old mine or something on the satellite. I'll try to get the Law-Enforcer-in-Chief as a reception committee. The only drawback is that we'll have to stand for hours ankle deep in ice-flakes listening to him recite a great long speech of official reproach. That fellow loves the sound of his own voice. Please try to get your father to keep his contrition response short and snappy. Can't I get you to change your mind, X? Why waste all your scholarship money?'

'You don't understand how serious it is,' X said. 'They've all become completely enchanted by the life-style here. They talk about nothing else. I've got to get them home. If I leave it much longer, I may not be able to get them aboard the raft at all! They've become so enraptured with certain things . . .'

'They do have rather nice trinkets and games and pastimes on that planet,' Lox said. 'What about you? Isn't there anything that you'll regret leaving behind?'

'Nothing!' X said. 'Nothing at all!'

But her hand closed upon the little coloured puzzle sphere in her skirt pocket.

ELEVEN

'This last day of school is to pass without incident, and afterwards you're all to come straight home and help me clear up the house. When it gets dark, we'll board the raft.'

Dovis burst into a fresh flood of tears. She had been crying almost continually since breakfast.

'Stop at once,' X said. 'You don't want to arrive back on Zyrgon with eyes like laser holes.'

'I don't want to arrive back on Zyrgon at all just yet! You don't understand anything!'

'I understand enough to know when my orders are being flouted. Just where is Father? I told him not to leave the house today.'

Aunt Hecla silently gestured to the message-pad on the kitchen table. X read: 'My presence is required at the Hybrid-Antelope and that's all there is to it, so there!'

There were other things scribbled at random on the pad: 'Twelve avocados, order sparkling wines, red roses long-stemmed variety for lady customers plus learn compliments in French to impress same; can Zeppy be trained to provide background dinner music when hibernation over; extensions – mezzanine floor plus red velvet carpet and chairs, see bank re: mortgage if Hecla can't raise money through Bingo. Don't tell X just yet.

P.S. Think up ways to postpone inevitable.'

'Father is wasting his time,' she said. 'We shan't even be having our evening meal at that ridiculous place. We'll be eating aboard the raft in transit. However, there's no harm in him tinkering about making a fool of himself at that restaurant all day if he chooses. I'll pick him up when it's time to go. Dovis and Qwrk, straighten your ties and unpin those silly ribbons from your blazers.'

'They're house colours for the Interhouse Aths,' said Dovis. 'Everyone wears them. You can nag and bully and lecture as much as you like, but I'm not taking them off. I'm not even going to walk to school with you either, on this last day! Come on, Qwrk!'

X stared at the slammed door, became aware of Aunt Hecla's gaze upon her and fought to regain her poise. 'Over-excitement on Dovis's part,' she said with dignity. 'I'd forgotten about the Interhouse Aths. Aunt, while I'm at school, I'll be glad if you'll start tidying. Take everything down and stack it in the hallway to be got rid of. We must leave this house as clean and empty as we found it, and I'll attend to the final details when I come home. I must go to school, because I have to take part in these Interhouse Aths as a team representative.'

'Teams?'

'Competing one against another. The team which wins the most points is awarded a prize. They have difficult events, like Zoomsleds, and I'm in a running event.'

Aunt Hecla looked even more interested. 'You can place a bet on for me, then, X, though I'll leave you to make a selection. I haven't been around to assess everyone's form and pick the likely winners. I could do with some extra currency.'

'You certainly could not! We're leaving tonight, and anyhow, all the money you did manage to amass here has been treacherously spent on violin lessons and illegal restaurants.'

'That was between your Father and me. He was going to pay me back at a very high rate once the restaurant took off.'

'It was still wrong of you to encourage him. He's been the most defiant one in the whole family about going back, and I'm certainly not looking forward to getting him aboard that raft.'

'X, why don't you let them stay a little longer?'

'It's my duty to break all these infatuations and get them back to Zyrgon.'

'I didn't know you were all that attached to Zyrgon. Messy place, you often complained to me when you came over to help with the herding. Everyone's so crazy about gambling and cheating and getting ahead by trickery. Even at that posh Knowledge Bank. One of those professor types turned up at my place once to write a thesis on granular ice, but it was a lot of nonsense. He didn't do any research. He spent all his time over on the other side of the satellite, hanging round that flashy resort where the old Klickscore Casino is. The night before he went back, he just bribed one of the herders to jot down a few details about the ice-flow, wrote it all up in iambic verse to make it look good, and went back to collect his promotion, frozen buttermilk wouldn't melt in his mouth! And what makes it worse is everyone pretending it doesn't exist, and acting outraged if anyone's found out.'

'I know all that, but Zyrgon's our home. It's my duty to keep them all there as a family unit.'

'You're much too young to be working as an Organizer,

anyhow,' Aunt Hecla grumbled. 'I told you so when you enrolled for that course, but you wouldn't listen. Your father's fault, too, not getting a warehouse robot to do the job, like most people. Anyway, X, you go off to school and don't worry about it, just for this last day. Would you like me to come along and sabotage the efforts of the others, so you can win?'

'They don't do things like that at Miss Brewster's school.'

'I could maybe knock up a flagon of rockshine and slip it to them disguised as tea. No one can run if they're full of rockshine.'

'I couldn't allow you to do anything like that. They regard these sports as very important. Their parents even come along to watch.'

'They make that much fuss about it?'

'Apparently. I'm going to feel conspicuous without any adult relatives there, but it can't be helped. I had to let Mother go to the boutique one last time. You know how sentimental she can be. Aunt Hecla, you will stay in the house, won't you, and not wander about all over town? I don't want to have to go looking for you when it's time to board the raft.'

'Get out of here, X,' Aunt Hecla said irritably. 'I'm too old to be organized like the others. I like to do things in my own way and in my own time.'

When X arrived at school, Jenny rushed to meet her with outspread arms. 'Oh, Charlotte, I'm so glad you're back! I know you didn't mean to sound so unfriendly when I called in. Mum said it was probably just the flu that made you sound like that. But you haven't got any green ribbons on your blazer! Here, have some of mine!'

X stepped awkwardly out of the circle of Jenny's arms.

She couldn't recall ever having been welcomed in such a lavish way after an absence. Whenever she'd returned from antelope round-ups, her household members would just say, 'Oh, there you are, X, would you take up the hem of this gown with Permapress?' Or, 'We've run out of protein and calcium envelopes, you'd better order some more.' Jenny's welcome lapped about her like sunlight.

'I was going to ring you up if you hadn't come today. About ice-skating tomorrow night at the new rink.'

'Ice-skating?'

'Haven't you ever been ice-skating before?'

X shook her head. She remembered the data about skating, which she'd read on the voyage. The illustrations for that sport had been rather captivating. It was strange that there was nothing like it on Zrygon, only those beastly sleds in the ice-season, trying to crowd each other off the spillway, sabotage and money changing hands . . . And you couldn't even see the drivers properly, huddled as they were into those little domed cabins, all goggles and furtiveness. Perhaps that was the reason why nobody had thought of ice-skating. Everyone on Zyrgon was too busy gambling and betting on the racing sleds. But she would much rather go to an ice-skating rink with Jenny Roland.

'That new rink's lovely,' Jenny said. 'And I'll teach you how to skate. You know, it's funny, Charlotte, but as soon as my brother Colin heard I was going to ask you, he invited himself along, too. He NEVER goes skating, usually. Know what I think? I think he's keen on you!'

Keen? What could Jenny mean by that? X decided to look it up in the PIC before she ventured into that rink, then remembered abruptly about tonight's departure.

'I won't be able to come skating,' she said. 'We shan't be here tomorrow. We're going away tonight, for good.'

'But that's terrible! You didn't tell me you were only going to be living here for a couple of weeks. Charlotte, I was looking forward to us being best friends . . .'

Best friends, that curious custom. On Zyrgon, no one had best friends, but rather a huge assortment of noisy, laughing acquaintances with whom one went gambling, to casino openings, to luncheons at one apartment after another.

X looked helplessly at Jenny, wondering why her spirits had billowed so suddenly and inexplicably when Jenny had made that remark about being best friends. And just as inexplicably plunged.

'I'll never see her again after today,' X thought. 'I shan't be able to write to her, converse with her over a beam, anything. It will be as though we never met each other at all. And it doesn't matter. Why should it? She's just a girl of my own age who happened to be sitting in the next desk at this ridiculous alien school. She'll forget about me in a week, as I shall about her, once I'm back on Zyrgon and busy with all my work. At the moment she's reacting emotionally. They all do, down here. They are very undignified people, with their emotions running wild and their reckless way of driving.'

She looked away from Jenny Roland to the trees lining the oval. Some of the leaves on the topmost branches were changing colour. She thought idly that those trees might be rather a splendid sight when they changed colour completely, if they matched the beautiful illustrations of autumn that she'd seen. There, she was becoming just as foolish as Dovis! She made her face carefully neutral.

124

'You don't even care!' Jenny said furiously. 'How can you be like that about it? You never said one word about going away, and now you don't even say you'll write or anything!'

'I shan't be able to write to you,' X said. 'You mustn't expect it.'

'At first, when you came, I thought you looked a bit lost and lonely. Even though you hid it so well and stood up to that awful Michelle and Dallas. I thought you were so interesting, not a bit like anyone else, and you seemed interested when I told you things ... Well, so much for that! I can see now it was all a big act! Well then, if you want to nick off casually like that without even looking a bit sorry, see if I care! I'm not even going to wish you luck in the four-hundred metres! I don't know why you even bothered turning up for that, if you're leaving. You're just plain stuck-up, that's what you are, Charlotte Jackson. You think you're too good for anyone, even to be their pen-friend!'

Jenny rushed away and became strenuously occupied in helping Miss Payne carry sports equipment to the oval. There was a gala atmosphere about the school, but X's heart was as heavy as metal. In mid-afternoon visitors began to arrive and the car park was filled with cars. The students were sent down to the oval, where X stood close to Dovis and Qwrk, forming a rather forlorn little family group. Everyone else seemed to have at least one parent present. Mrs Roland waved to her across the rails, but Jenny was pretending that X didn't exist.

'At least you won't have to worry if you don't win,' Dovis said tersely. 'You're determined that we won't be here tomorrow. So at least you'll avoid Retribution from the people in Green House.'

'I don't think they use Retribution against the losers. There wasn't any mention of it at the training selection.'

'They didn't let the prep grade enter for anything,' Qwrk said. 'It's discrimination on the grounds of age, as I pointed out to Miss Delaney. Next Interhouse Aths . . .'

'Which doesn't concern us because we won't be here,' X said crossly.

'Qwrk won't be allowed to enter next year,' Dovis said. 'They'd be worried he'd hurt his hands. Even though he's not learning violin through the school, Miss Brewster still treats him as a resident prodigy. I shan't be in the Interhouse Aths next year either.'

'Obviously you won't. You'll be a member of the Cosmic Fliers.'

'Oh, them! I haven't thought about them for ages. I didn't mean that, anyhow. I meant that next year I could be editor of the school magazine instead. Miss Rogers has been very impressed with my poetry . . .'

'Dovis!'

'Do you mind not having any adult relatives here to watch you run, like everyone else!' Qwrk put in tactfully. 'If you like, Astrella and I can age-simulate.'

'That won't be necessary. I'm here only because my name is on the list, and I don't want to leave anything unfinished. I like things to be in order. It doesn't matter to me if people watch this race or if they don't.'

Miss Payne beckoned her, and X realized that the four-hundred metres was to start very soon. 'Here comes the representative of the Slimeys,' Michelle said, and X remembered that that was what they called anyone in Green House. Michelle, however, had made it sound like a personal insult. X ignored her and looked across at the visiting spectators lining the rails. They were watching other events, glowing with pride because their daughters had been chosen to compete. X felt suddenly desolate there with no one interested in her success or failure.

'Haven't your parents turned up to watch the sports?' Dallas said. 'Are they ashamed of you or something?'

'They haven't turned up because they know Charlotte will run last,' Michelle said. 'Very tactful of them, I'd say.'

'Maybe she hasn't got any parents.'

'Maybe she just grew on a gooseberry bush.'

'On a nut tree, you mean,' said Dallas.

X gazed across the rail at Jenny Roland. The distance between them could have been bridged by two out-stretched hands, one linking with the other. But it seemed instead like the vast distance between this world and Zyrgon. The look in Jenny's eyes made it so.

'Entrants for the four-hundred metres, take your places at the starting line,' said Miss Payne, and X lined up with the other girls.

'Waste of time, you being here,' Michelle whispered nastily. 'It was only a fluke you beat us at the trials. Bet you won't last this distance!'

Someone fired a gun nearby, and X, extremely startled and shocked, looked around to see who had done such a dangerous thing. She had learned about such weapons from watching television. But she found that it was evidently the signal to begin the race. The other four girls had already leaped forward, and she ran after them comfortably, not hurrying very much. Two were running much too fast to sustain energy for such a long distance. She listened to the shouting from the rails, but none of it was for her. She seemed to be running within a small forgotten space, a distance behind the other four, but eventually the two impetuous girls, with no reserves of energy left, fell back and she passed them. She glanced at Michelle and Dallas, a long way ahead.

Suddenly she heard her name acclaimed, in a voice louder than anyone else's. She stared towards that large voice, scarcely recognizing Aunt Hecla who now looked so much like a PIC model of a dignified elderly lady. Except, X thought doubtfully, elderly ladies probably didn't yell at the top of their voices or thump the person standing next to them on the back with excitement.

X caught up with Dallas. In passing, she turned and stuck out her tongue. She didn't know what made her do such a frivolous thing, realizing that it wasn't a polite gesture and should be avoided at all costs. But it felt immensely satisfying. She looked ahead at Michelle, who ran like a machine. X imagined herself back on Zyrgon's satellite, rounding up that fiendish, irritating little pest Zeppy. Michelle was every bit as irritating.

X caught up, ran side by side with Michelle for some distance, then casually sprinted ahead and stayed there. There was a white tape, and as she ran into it, she heard her name called over a loudspeaker: 'Charlotte Jackson, Green House, First Place.'

People, unbelievably, crowded around to congratulate her. On Zyrgon, if you came first in anything, you always had to dodge the wrathful losers with their barrage of insults and their angry backers. It wasn't really healthy to win anything on Zyrgon, and people only competed for the prize money and the excitement of danger. She remembered all the churlish anonymous letters she'd received after winning the Organizer Scholarship. But to her astonishment, even Michelle said, 'Congratulations, Charlotte,' when she finally caught up. Not graciously, but not with malice, either. There was even a degree of respect in her voice.

Miss Payne was hanging something about X's neck. Some sort of medal on a blue ribbon. 'You're an asset to your team, Charlotte,' Miss Payne was saying above the noise, for Aunt Hecla's voice had been joined by others. 'Naturally you'll be in the school team for the Interschool Competitions later this term. Congratulations for winning the medal. You certainly deserved it.'

Interschool Competitions? School team? They were obviously significant, judging by the expressions of the girls standing nearby, who looked awed and impressed. X resolved to check any available data.

Then she remembered that she would have no need to consult the PIC ever again after tonight. It would have to be jettisoned with everything else. They mustn't be found with anything incriminating when they landed on Zyrgon.

Not even her medal.

TWELVE

'I intend to have a thorough search once we're airborne. Nothing at all is to arrive on Zyrgon except ourselves.'

'If Dovis can take a photograph of David Carruthers, then I can take my violin,' Qwrk said stubbornly.

Dovis turned red with guilt and defiance. X pounced. The confiscated photograph bore little resemblance to Dovis's infatuated description of that boy. The picture showed large ears and an inane smile, but Dovis still put up a fiercely possessive fight. X found herself sitting on the floor with one ear humming from a blow and the marks of fingernails on her wrist while Dovis replaced the photograph in her pocket. 'I don't care if I do come out in green spots,' Dovis said recklessly. 'No one will see me on that boring trip home, anyhow.'

X rose and put herself to rights, repressing an urge to fly at Dovis and box her ears. She knew she musn't jeopardize dignity by physical fighting. 'Attacking an Organizer is a very serious offence,' she pointed out. 'When we're back on Zyrgon, I won't allow you to go to any underwater concerts for a whole three lunar months.'

'I don't care about that, either. What's an underwater concert compared to a cricket match? I never want to go anywhere ever again. When I get back I intend to stay in the modular and starve myself to death with David's photograph beside me. You'll have it on your conscience.'

'I'll let you keep that picture during the voyage, since you're being so emotional about it, and Qwrk may keep his violin for the same reason, but before we orbit Zyrgon, violin and photograph will be got rid of. The authorities will inspect the raft when we land and I shouldn't have to remind you that they mustn't find anything. This planet is completely out of bounds, and we'd all get detention in spite of the bribe. Now, stop this unruly behaviour AT ONCE and help me clear the house.'

When all the furniture and clothing had been gathered into the main room, she ordered Dovis to bulk-kinetize it into outer space. Dovis's lack of enthusiasm was obvious. Almost immediately, several objects popped back – a school tie, Qwrk's pink ruffled bed, some music tapes. 'I can't help it!' Dovis wailed. 'The whole situation is just too poignant!'

'If you don't do a thorough job, I'll change my mind about letting you have that photograph to look at on the trip,' X threatened, and when everything had vanished properly, she removed the wall mural. Mother sniffed quietly while it was being erased.

'Come on, you lot, cheer up,' Aunt Hecla said uncomfortably. 'Anyone would think you were being forced to listen to one of Mrs Gombaldu's singing recitals. All this misery is giving me the creeps! You don't see me standing about with a face like a glacier, do you?'

'It's different for you,' Mother said. 'You don't mind where you are, and you aren't having to give up a half-ownership of a boutique, either! Oh, Andrea's going to think so badly of me when I don't turn up tomorrow or ever again!'

X remained aloof from everyone's emotive leave-taking. She put the keys on a kitchen bench in the bare and spotless house for Mr Herring to find when the lease expired.

'Now, Dovis, kinetize Father and Zeppy back from that restaurant,' she ordered briskly. 'It's time we were leaving.'

'It wouldn't be respectful,' said Dovis. 'The girls at school would never kinetize their fathers anywhere. You don't treat fathers like that on this planet. You're just going to have to walk to the restaurant yourself and collect him.'

'We'll all walk to the restaurant and from there to the raft,' X said. 'I'm not letting anyone out of my sight for one minute till we're aboard.'

When they were all outside, she shut the front door on the house's emptiness and set off down Renmark Street, not looking back in case anyone had succumbed to tears. She listened to the sound of footsteps, slow and unwilling footsteps, but at least they were following.

'You can't blame them, X,' Aunt Hecla whispered. 'Bound to be a few red eyes, leaving a pretty planet like this one. You really should have let them have a few more weeks, you know. Your timing was right off, my girl.'

'Don't lecture me, Aunt Hecla. I know what I'm doing! I won the Community Centre scholarship for Organizing, didn't I?'

They passed houses with windows softly lit in the gathering dusk. X thought of the people gathered behind those windows, having their evening meal. And afterwards, those family groups would set about their leisurely evening schedules, watch TV, talk with one another, plan outings to ice-skating rinks . . .

'Sentimentality,' she told herself sharply. 'This inefficient, alien way of life has nothing to do with me. It will be good to leave such a maudlin planet and return to Zyrgon.'

They passed their school. 'Miss Brewster's school,' she corrected brusquely. There was the oval, and although she forced her eyes to look straight ahead, she heard in her mind the sound of people clapping and voices calling out her name. How strange that a talent for running was considered remarkable enough to deserve an award. Instinctively, her hand rose to clutch the medal on its ribbon about her neck. It would have to be ejected, with Dovis's photograph and Qwrk's violin, before the raft landed on Zyrgon. And why wait till then? Why not just drop it into the nearest litter bin right now, and set a good example to the others? During Organizing training she'd listened to countless lectures about setting good examples, and written dozens of assignments using that topic as a theme. Why, then, was it so difficult to put into practice? There was a rubbish bin just ahead, at the start of the shopping centre.

But before she could prove her emotional superiority by getting rid of the medal, the others caught up, passed her without stopping, and went through the door of a building. 'Your father's restaurant,' Aunt Hecla explained. 'We all had afternoon-tea here one day when you were sick in bed, that's how they know where it is.'

X pushed open the door. It had a sign saying: *The Hybrid-Antelope; Mortimer Jackson, Manager and Chef.* Inside the walls were white and there was dark wood-panelling on the ceiling. The tables were spread with checked cloths, set for a meal, and there was a wonderful smell of food being cooked in the adjoining kitchen. X thought of the provisions aboard the raft, hard little emergency envelopes in unattractive colours. This restaurant was charming, the sort of place where one could enjoy having a meal, but she set that thought aside and looked sternly around for Mortimer Jackson, Manager and Chef.

Zeppy was displayed on a pedestal next to the cash register. He lay, deep in hibernation, in a fluff of ringlets with his hooves tucked up. Every time he breathed, and you could scarcely tell he was breathing, there was a faint ripple of little silver bells. X looked more closely, for something odd had happened to Zeppy since she'd last seen him. His fleece had changed from its normal silvery white into bands of striated colour.

Aunt Hecla stood as though mesmerized, gaping at him. She picked up a ringlet and ran it through her fingers. 'Oh, my!' she said. 'Will you just look at this! Maybe it's the diet he's had down here, or atmospheric pressure or something. X, I could swear it's permanent colour, too, and machine washable!'

'Whatever it is, we can't take him back looking like that,' X said, exasperated by the new problem. 'The authorities would know something funny has been going on. You'll have to shear him once we're aboard the raft and we'll jettison the fleece.'

'You don't shear hybrids while they're hibernating!' Aunt Hecla said scornfully. 'They're very sensitive creatures. Anyhow, nothing can make me give up this fleece after all my years of trying to grow colour. You can't expect it of me!'

'Then I'll steer the raft over the satellite before we land on Zyrgon, and you can drop Zeppy down by chute.'

'The ranch air might turn his fleece back to white! X, I'm not going to risk it, and take that as final! There's only one thing for me to do, and that's stay behind. Dovis could easily kinetize a female hybrid back here for mating. Oh, just fancy, I might have a whole flock of multi-coloureds in a couple of solar years.'

'Aunt Hecla, you can't possibly stay down here by yourself! What about the ranch, for a start?'

'To tell the truth, child, that ranch is really getting too much for me, specially in the cold season. Anyhow, I've had offers for it. There's a syndicate that wants to turn it into a retirement home for pensioned-off Organizers. You know those poor doddery old things no one wants when their families are grown-up and independent . . . oops, sorry, that's a bit tactless, isn't it? But you don't have to worry about me, X. I'll earn enough from Bingo to live on, and I'll just take over that house you were renting until I can find another with a little bit of grazing land around it. Dovis will have to get the keys out, though, and the PIC back from space. I'll need some information on local weaving and spinning, only this time I'll keep my business scaled down. Just as a sort of nice little hobby-farm. You know, X, I'm really looking forward to it.'

X realized that no mere order on her part would get Aunt Hecla aboard the raft with everyone else, so she went into the kitchen to find Father. He was wearing the tall white cap and the apron, and was busy at a stove crammed with things simmering gently in pots. He stood in a fragrant spicy cloud.

'You must leave that and help me,' X said. 'Aunt Hecla has taken it into her head to stay down here and breed rainbow hybrids! You'll have to come and speak to her.'

'Not right now,' Father said absently. 'I'm in the middle

of a very critical manoeuvre. Why do you always get into such a state, X? Whatever it is must wait, because I'm just about to serve dinner.'

The white cap made him look unusually tall and serious. It was almost like a uniform, not as glamorous as the Space Shuttle of course, but in its own way, just as striking. He seemed to possess a new and stately distinction, standing there in command of the stove. It suddenly occurred to X that there was a similarity between Qwrk playing his violin and Father so engrossed in preparing a meal. Both wore identical expressions, as though the outside world and its cares had dwindled to something very unimportant. Father looked happy. Even more so than when he'd won the final big lottery, the one which had plunged their household into trouble and exile. That other happiness had been mingled with guilt, but Father certainly didn't look guilty now. He just looked completely and utterly content.

'I could postpone departure until we have a meal,' X decided. 'If everyone has a pleasant meal before we board the raft, perhaps there'll be less friction. And it will certainly give me a chance to think what to do about Aunt Hecla. We'll have to try and make up the lost time when we orbit Zyrgon, but if we can't, the Law Enforcer will just have to wait with his reception speech. Perhaps being unpunctual every now and then isn't such a great matter, anyhow.'

'Very well, Father,' she said. 'I suppose it would be a pity if the food you've prepared goes to waste. I'll give you permission to serve dinner.'

She expected humble gratitude for her generosity, but to her surprise, Father gave her a push, and not a gentle one, through the swing doors and into the dining room. 'I can't have you underfoot in my kitchen while I'm serving up,' he said crossly. 'Sit down somewhere and stop being such a little pest.'

X, outraged but silent, sat down opposite Dovis.

'That's how Lynne's father talks to her,' Dovis said with interest. 'How clever of Father to have learned the correct idiom.'

'He'll have to unlearn it on the voyage,' X said, but her annoyance ebbed when Father began to serve the meal. They were to have Veal and Broccoli Consommé; Curried Cream Scallops; Chicken and Champagne Mousse; Tournedos with Mustard Béarnaise; Sherried Mint Peas, Potatoes Romanoff, Artichokes with Almond and Lychee Salad; and Hot Raspberry Soufflé with Marsala Ice-cream. X thought of Zyrgonese luncheons with their horrid, ostentatious little crystal cakes that tasted of nothing.

'We have our own violinist at this restaurant,' Father said with pride. 'George, some dinner music, please.'

Qwrk picked up his violin and began to play, but the music seemed unbearably perceptive and bittersweet, as though Qwrk were translating into sound everyone's sad feelings about leaving. X found herself unable to eat the wonderful food before her. It suddenly tasted as unpalatable as crystal cakes. She put down her fork and looked around the table. Everyone else had stopped eating, too.

'An Organizer must show fortitude, dignity and firmness of mind in every action,' she thought, remembering the lectures at Community Centre. 'An Organizer is solely responsible for all major decisions. An Organizer is in full control of the family unit at all times. But they forgot to tell us the most basic thing of all,' she thought miserably. 'Being an Organizer is the loneliest job in the galaxy and I hate it! I wish I'd never wanted to be one. It's nothing but a pain in the neck and I wish I could get out of it and just be ME!'

'George, this is supposed to be a special celebration dinner,' Father said.

'What's there to celebrate?'

'X winning the four-hundred metres, of course. Aunt Hecla mentally televised the whole race while it was taking place and relayed it on to me. I only wish I'd been there in person to watch.'

'I don't know any medal music, but I'll compose some,' Qwrk said. His new music sparkled zestfully, but X felt as bleak as a roof garden in winter.

Father went into the kitchen and returned with a magnificent cake which blazed with light from four-hundred candles. 'One for each metre you ran today,' he explained. 'I was hoping for the opportunity to make such a cake, but nobody's due for a solar birthday yet. So Aunt Hecla's report came as a delightful surprise.'

X had seen the PIC data on birthday cakes, and had thought it a very strange custom indeed, but such a cake in reality wasn't strange. It was beautiful, and very touching.

'You must blow out the candles and make a wish,' Father said. 'That's what they do here.'

But suddenly, without any assistance from X, the little flames flickered and died one by one.

'I don't think it's very grateful showing off your powers at a time like this,' Dovis said reproachfully. 'We all know you've got them, for you never tire of demonstrations, but that's no reason to spoil Father's surprise.'

'I wasn't doing any such thing!' X cried, unable to check the emotion in her voice. It somehow seemed terribly important that they should understand that she hadn't been showing off at all. Not this time, and not with a spectacular cake that had been made specially to commemorate something she'd done. 'I certainly didn't make the candles go out. I think it's Lox trying to get through on a thought beam. He always misjudges the distance.'

She did her best to compose her mind for contact. Lox appeared to be generating a lot of power from his own end, and there was a sense of urgency about it. His beam skittered about all over the place, first focusing on Zeppy and making him wriggle bad-temperedly in his sleep, then skipping away from Zeppy to the ceiling and getting stuck there. X assembled her powers and plucked the end of Lox's beam out of the air-vent.

'Phew!' Lox said. 'I haven't had to get up one of those things for a long time. I'd forgotten how tiring they are.' He sounded frazzled, out of breath, and decidedly aggressive. 'There's been a complication. I've been put to a lot of inconvenience, and I strongly resent it.'

'Couldn't you get the central landing-bay?' X asked. 'There wasn't any need to set up a special beam to let me know about that. I'll still get the raft down somehow.'

'It's not that at all,' Lox said. 'I wish you wouldn't take charge of conversations, X, in that bossy way you have. It's about your so-called Scholarship money.'

Father, who had been setting out cups, suddenly halted. He looked, X decided, suspiciously ill at ease.

'What about my Scholarship money?' she asked Lox. 'It's in the Community Centre office files with my examination results, as I told you. And I've already given you the safety-casket number. All you had to do was break into the office after hours, remove the money and give it to a Law Enforcer as a bribe. Nothing simpler. What could possibly have gone wrong?'

'I didn't collect it personally; I told the Enforcer he could. It didn't seem to make any difference whether I broke in and handed the money over, or if he broke in and collected it himself.'

'It's a question of ethics,' X said. 'A matter of finesse. You shouldn't ask people to steal their own bribes ...'

'I was busy,' Lox said sullenly. 'I had an appointment for a pre-betrothal portrait and I wanted to look my best, not have a picture taken in a uniform all crumpled from breaking and entering. And as it happens, I still haven't had that portrait taken because there's been such a turmoil. You ought to be ashamed of yourself, X, doing something like that.'

'Doing something like what? I don't understand ...'

'There's no need to sound so innocent. That Enforcer had a little snoop through your test results while he was there; you know how they always do that automatically, like breathing. I never dreamed that your affairs wouldn't be in impeccable order.'

'But they are! The Principal kept my file specially, as an example of how any student who put her mind to it could get straight A's in every single subject in the final testing. Of course my papers are in order! I watched them being stamped with the official seal and put away with my money for when I reached retirement age. They made a little ceremony out of it and everyone in my study group was called in to witness. Has someone sabotaged ...'

'Would anyone like some coffee to go with this cake?' Father asked loudly, clattering cups and saucers on the table. X frowned him to silence.

'I'm not talking about sabotage!' Lox yelled into the silence. 'I'm talking about CHEATING! The Enforcer ran all your tests through his pocket-scan and picked up the falsifications right away! You know very well you didn't deserve any of those A's. Every single test result was rigged! Why, you barely scraped through most of them, and some you failed altogether. Mind you, the Law Enforcer was impressed by the high quality of the forgery. To the naked eye, he said, it was hardly different from the real thing.'

'Oh, X!' Mother said, distressed. 'I just hope Mrs Gombaldu doesn't get to hear of this!'

'Of course she will!' Lox said. 'There's an order out for X's detention. Fifteen years she'll get at the very least. No Organizer has ever falsified their test papers to win a scholarship before, it's completely unheard of! I know it happens all the time in the other faculties, but not Organizing. They're supposed to be upright and honest and set a good example to everyone else, so don't expect me to be waiting on the tarmac when you land. I don't want to be seen in public with you, X. Jady would be most upset if my picture got into the *Morning Star* connected with anything so unsavoury.'

'Well!' thought X through her consternation and shocked dismay. 'What a nerve that Lox has! Anyone would think he'd never in his whole life done anything underhand!'

Incredulously she demanded, 'You mean you wouldn't stand by me if I got Detention?'

'I'm after promotion, now that I'm betrothed. Jady and I have seen a wonderful snobby apartment over by the casino, only the rent is very expensive. As it is, I had to do some very fast talking to convince them I didn't know anything about the way you manipulated those marks. When you land, I'd appreciate it if your family doesn't mention my name or claim more than passing acquaintance.'

'How could I ever have liked Lox?' X wondered, listening to the gigantic self-interest and pride in his voice.

'So, what do you want to do? It's both you *and* your father they're after now. Of course, you could land on the satellite instead and hide on your aunt's ranch. No one's likely to go there until the ice melts. You could stay there and shiver and hope that the Government changes before the thaw. But I can't help you any longer.'

Lox berating her in that detestable voice, it could hardly be borne! Lox, whom she'd admired in secret all these years! There was certainly nothing admirable about him now!

An arm slipped unexpectedly around her shoulders. 'You leave X alone!' Father growled down the beam. 'She didn't cheat, anyhow, it was me. She had her heart set on that Organizing course and she was only fair to middling at it, anyone could see. So I sneaked into the Community Centre and rearranged the final score a little. The scan they have there isn't so different from a Klickscore counter, when all's said and done. And I'll thank you to get off this beam now, Lox, and leave poor X in peace to recover. She's had a nasty shock.'

'I've had a worse one! It still hasn't changed the situation here, and X still hasn't told me what she plans to do. Are you all landing here as arranged, or going to the satellite, or what?'

'X shouldn't have to suffer Detention for something she didn't even do. They won't believe me if I own up to it, either, no one ever believes those public confessions people make on Zyrgon. And the satellite is out, because Hecla doesn't own that ranch anymore. During my Tournedos with Mustard Béarnaise, she made mind contact with a Zyrgonese syndicate and arranged a sale, money to be collected at some future, unspecified date.'

142

'Well, if you're planning to stay where you are, I wouldn't bet on your chances much longer. I'm afraid that I let slip about your space-raft, and as it's obsolete government property, all they have to do is check their files for the signal number, put a location beam on it, and zoom in on you. I expect they'll be down to pick you all up in a couple of days' time.'

'We'll decide what to do after . . . after we finish our cake,' Father said bravely. 'We'll be in touch.'

'I prefer that you didn't. I really don't want to be involved.'

And without farewells of any kind, Lox terminated the beam as abruptly as a slammed door.

'I'm sorry about all this, X,' Father said ruefully.

'I should have suspected,' she said. 'I thought at the time that getting such high marks in the final testing was odd, when I knew perfectly well I was only average in class. I suppose I fooled myself into believing. You see, I had to have something, too, like Qwrk at Knowledge Bank and Dovis . . .'

'I couldn't bear you to fail,' Father said. 'You were so determined about that Organizing course.'

'There didn't seem to be anything else I could choose. I was so hopeless at everything else, flying and designing Wear . . . everything.'

'There's one thing you can do very well,' Qwrk said. 'And that's shift objects in and out of air pockets. Even large objects, such as illegal space-rafts.'

'I'll do my best,' X said, and drew every last shred of her powers together, knowing that this was going to be a formidable task. She shut her eyes and concentrated unwaveringly on the raft, hidden in the field where they'd landed. The raft was so bulky that shock waves hit

143

her as the transferral took place, but when she recovered, she knew that there was nothing left in that field except a semi-circle of fuel leaks. Any location beam set up by the Law Enforcers would lead straight to the chilly south pasture of Aunt Hecla's ranch, soon to be a retirement home. Perhaps when they located the raft, they'd leave it there as an outdoor shelter for those poor old pensioned-off Organizers who'd never had any enjoyment out of life.

There was nothing left of her powers, either, after that immense effort.

'Not that I had many to start with,' she thought without regret. 'All those A's on the final test can't alter the fact that I was totally unsuitable to be an Organizer, with no real skills for it. And thank goodness for that!'

'I think I'll make a pot of tea,' said Father. 'I know coffee's smarter, but didn't the PIC say somewhere that tea is what everyone here drinks in a crisis?'

'It doesn't really feel like a crisis,' said Dovis. 'It feels more like a beginning. But whatever it is, I hope no one will ever pester me again to do any more boring old kinetics.'

'Only just one more time,' X said apologetically. 'You'll have to get all our things back, because we'll be needing them, but at the same time I want you to get rid of a lot of silly pictures I forgot about.'

'Pictures?'

'They're nothing important. There's also another thing. You're all going to have to organize yourselves from now on, starting from tomorrow. I won't have time. I'm going out tomorrow.'

'But X, you never go out!' Mother said.

'I'm going ice-skating with my friend Jenny Roland and a very nice boy called Colin,' Charlotte Jackson said triumphantly.

DOLPHIN ISLAND
Arthur C. Clarke

When an intercontinental hovership breaks down outside his house, Johnny Clifton stows away on board, happy to escape from his life with Aunt Martha.

RACSO AND THE RATS OF NIMH
Leslie Jane Conly

A sequel to MRS FRISBY AND THE RATS OF NIMH in which Mrs Frisby and her son, Timothy, help in the fight to save their valley from flooding.

THE PRIME MINISTER'S BRAIN
Gillian Cross

The fiendish 'hypnotiser', first encountered in THE DEMON HEADMASTER, now plans to gain control of No. 10 Downing Street and lure the Prime Minister into his evil control.

SLADE

John Tully

Slade has a mission – to investigate life on Earth. When Eddie discovers the truth about Slade he gets a whole lot more adventure than he bargained for.

THE HOUNDS OF THE MORRIGAN

Pat O'Shea

When the Great Queen Morrigan, evil creature from the world of Irish mythology, returns to destroy the world, Pidge and Brigit are the children chosen to thwart her. How they go about it makes an hilarious, moving story, full of totally original and unforgettable characters.

COLIN'S FANTASTIC VIDEO ADVENTURE

Kenneth Oppel

A lively and bizarre story in which Colin, a fanatical player of video games, discovers in his pocket two spacemen from his favourite game.

RAGING ROBOTS AND UNRULY UNCLES

Margaret Mahy

A wonderfully original story about wicked Uncle Jasper and his law-abiding brother Julian, whose children are driven away by two terrible robots!

EXILES OF COLSEC

Douglas Hill

Thrilling science fiction from a master of the genre. An unruly mixture of drop-out kids crash-land on an alien planet. The unlikely group has been chosen to colonize the planet . . .

THE CHILDREN OF MORROW

H.M. Hoover

Brought up in a world of fear in an oppressive society, two children decide to seek a better life. An exciting tale of the future.